DARE TO LOVE A MARQUESS

SOLDIERS AND SWEETHEARTS (BOOK 3)

ROSE PEARSON

DARE TO LOVE A MARQUESS

Soldiers and Sweethearts

(Book 3)

By

Rose Pearson

DARE TO LOVE A MARQUESS

PROLOGUE

It had all happened so fast.

Frederick, Marquess of Stratham, winced, closing his eyes as the memories came at him thick and fast. He did not welcome them but, at the same time, did not push them away. The heat of that moment seemed to sear his skin all over again, the sounds of the men next to him, their horses screaming, coming into his ears as though he were standing on the battlefield at that very moment.

His skin prickled and his breathing grew quick, but still, Frederick let the memories wash over him. He had not been able to remember such a moment for a long time and now that his memories had finally returned to him, he did not want to forget, did not want to ignore those who had fought alongside him... and those who had died. A chill stole over him and he shuddered violently, remembering how he had fallen, how pain had seemed to pour into his very bones. Swords and bayonets had pierced him, both in his side and across his face, but it was the fall from his horse that had knocked him unconscious. He could not remember anything after that, save for waking up in a hospital tent where he had been ministered to by one of the army's surgeons.

Opening his eyes, Frederick rose to his feet, pushing himself out of his chair. Making his way to the window, he planted both hands on his hips and let out a long, slow breath, trying to steady himself. His eyes found their way to where the bottle of brandy was sitting, but Frederick shook his head firmly. It would not do for his staff to find him in a state of panic, nor in a state of inebriation! This moment would pass, and he would soon be himself again.

The flickering candlelight illuminated his features as he looked at his reflection in the glass of the window. Absently, he lifted his hand and let his fingers run down over his scar. It began near to the corner of his eye and ran to the bottom of his jaw, meaning that, even if he had wished to, he could not hide it.

I am not a vain man.

Frederick dropped his hand and once more took in another long breath, letting it fill his lungs and lift his chest. Yes, he had returned to London rather than staying with the army, but that did not mean that he had any intention of seeking a wife. He had responsibilities and duties here; obligations that would keep him entirely occupied. Those sympathetic to the French had to be discovered, those working *for* the French had to suffer the consequences of their treachery. And he still had to make certain that the invasion that he knew the French spoke of never came to fruition. He had no time to consider any young ladies, to let himself call on them for afternoon tea and such! All of his thoughts and all of his efforts had to be solely focused on the war and his efforts towards securing England's victory. Therefore, it did not matter whether or not the ladies of the *ton* would react badly to his now injured face.

Then why does it bother me so?

Frederick grimaced, turning away from the window, and telling himself that he ought not to be so foolish. Anyone who considered him a lesser gentleman now, simply because of his scar, was not someone that Frederick would wish to have as an acquaintance. Yes, there would always be whispers and gossip about him, but he had to simply ignore all such things and continue as he had intended. Any words which were spoken of him, any whispers which were spread behind his back, had to simply be ignored.

A tap at the door indicated that one of his staff had arrived and Frederick called for them to enter, glad of the distraction.

"My Lord." The butler inclined his head. "Lord Ware has written to you."

Frederick grasped the note quickly, murmuring a word of thanks before dismissing the butler. Breaking the seal, he allowed himself to read the first few lines, before moving to his overstuffed armchair. Settling into it, Frederick continued to read, smiling to himself as he learned of how Lord and Lady Ware were enjoying their wedding trip.

'I write also to inform you that I have discovered that those we seek to reveal are doing all they can to support an invasion by the French onto our shores,' Frederick read, his brow furrowing. *'Lady Ware and I happened to come across some particular information during our travels and thought it of the utmost importance that you became aware of it just as soon as was possible. I know that the Duke of Abernyte and yourself are working hard to discover who else within the ton is aiding the French, but I fear that there is even more urgency than we had previously thought. My informant states that the invasion will be by the end of the Season, and*

that, should they be successful, the French will make their way to London with every intention of taking power from us by force. The meeting which we had hoped to infiltrate would, I expect, have revealed to us those who are involved in organizing such an endeavor. I wish you every success, Lord Stratham, and beg you to forgive me for being away at this present, most difficult time. Yours, Etc.,'

Frederick ran one hand over his brow, his mind turning over all that he had read. Lord Ware need not apologize, certainly, for even though there was a good deal going on at present, it was only right that a gentleman is permitted to enjoy his wedding trip with his new wife! It was not that sentiment that made him frown, however, but the realization that he was just as far away from discovering the truth as ever. Yes, they had already taken into custody a few gentlemen from the *ton* who were involved in supporting the French in their endeavors, but it seemed now that they had not got to the heart of it. Frederick closed his eyes, leaned back in his chair, and let out a heavy sigh. They had been so very close to being able to infiltrate the group of gentlemen who met to co-ordinate the aid which they had been bringing to the French, but it had not quite worked out as they had planned. Now, however, Frederick felt a fresh determination fill him as he considered all that Lord Ware had told him. He, alongside the Duke of Abernyte, would find those who sought to aid the French and would make certain that their efforts came to naught. Somehow, he would get to the heart of them and rip it apart, bringing them all to their knees. The invasion would not take place and England's shores would be safe.

"I am determined." Frederick let his fingers run down over his scar once more, feeling his heart fill with a new resolve. All that he had fought for, all that he had endured, and all that he had lost would not be allowed to stand for nothing. Those who sought England's downfall would, instead, find themselves lost in failure. He nodded grimly to himself, his free hand clenching into a fist. "This time," he said aloud, his voice low and dark, "we will succeed entirely."

CHAPTER ONE

"That is very kind of you to say, Lord Newton. I am certain that my daughter thinks it a great compliment."

Lady Georgina Fielding sighed inwardly and held her mother's gaze for a moment, fully aware of the grim look which was being sent her way, but finding that it did not unsettle her in the least.

"A very kind compliment, certainly," she murmured, barely glancing at Lord Newton as he beamed back at her in evident delight. "Thank you, Lord Newton."

She watched as her mother's shoulders dropped just a fraction, evidently a little relieved that Georgina had answered in both a calm and genteel manner. Georgina rolled her eyes and looked away from both Lord Newton and her mother, finding herself utterly bored with all that she was expected to do. This was her second Season and, whilst her father had very little interest in all that Georgina was doing, her mother was seemingly quite determined that Georgina should become acquainted with every single gentleman in all of London! Georgina was growing weary of it for, whilst it was a blessing to be considered so *very* popular by those in the *ton*, it gave her no opportunity to actually consider any gentleman specifically. Every time she so much as mentioned one to her mother, Lady Kingham would shake her head and state some fault or other that particular gentleman had, and then declare that Georgina could make a much better match.

Georgina knew full well that her mother secretly hoped that Georgina would soon become acquainted with a Duke and that she might find a suitable husband in such a refined gentleman, but as yet, Georgina had been unable to achieve such an acquaintance. Being the daughter of an Earl, Georgina would have been more than contented to marry a gentleman of a similar rank, but Lady Kingham would not relent from pressing her to consider someone of a higher standing than herself. Lord Newton, it seemed, was someone that her mother thought to be suitable for Georgina, as regarded his title and his wealth, but Georgina was not particularly interested. Lord Newton appeared to be rather older than she and, besides which, she found his lack of manners to be entirely unappealing. Lord Newton had not only drunk more tea than was expected but had eaten the entirety of their refreshments without even considering whether or not Georgina or Lady Kingham might wish for something to eat! She glanced back at him, seeing the crumbs which were lying about him on the carpet, as well as the ones on his knees, and found herself recoiling inwardly. She did not want to have such a slovenly gentleman for a husband, no matter his rank!

"I am certain that my daughter would be glad to save you a dance, Lord Newton!"

Georgina spun her head back around to glare fiercely at her mother, who merely gave her a small, victorious smile as though she knew that Georgina would immediately protest – but also that she could not do so aloud, given their company.

"Oh, how wonderful!" Lord Newton exclaimed, turning to face Georgina, his plump face a little redder than before. "I should very much like to have the waltz, Lady Georgina." A slightly uncertain look came into his eyes, his smile sliding away. "That is, if you would be willing to... what I mean to say is, so long as you are *permitted* to dance the waltz."

His gaze turned to Lady Kingham, who immediately laughed and waved a hand, as though to state that Georgina had always been permitted to dance such an intimate dance as the waltz!

"That is very..." Georgina hesitated, having been about to say 'kind' but realizing that she had already used that word a number of times. "Forward of you, Lord Newton," she continued, all too aware of the shock which poured into his expression at her choice of words. "You not only ask me to save you a dance at tomorrow evening's Ball, but you also beg of me to save you one dance in particular!"

She tried to laugh, aware that her mother was now glaring at her in a most disconcerting manner, but telling herself that she need not be concerned over it. After all, it was not as though Lady Kingham were the one who would be dancing with Lord Newton! The last thing Georgina wanted was to give Lord Newton any encouragement whatsoever, for she did not think herself at all interested in furthering their acquaintance.

"Why, Lady Georgina," Lord Newton replied, his eyes still a little wide. "That is only because I am very eager indeed for your company."

Georgina knew what she ought to say, knew what her

mother expected her to say but, looking back at Lord Newton and seeing the hopeful expectation in his eyes, Georgina knew that she could not.

She could not simply remain proper and genteel, saying all of the right things and not permitting herself to listen to her heart and stand her ground. No, she determined, silently. No, she would be honest with Lord Newton, regardless of what it might cost her. The *ton* ought to know her for who she really was – a young lady who was quite determined to make her own future, rather than being forced into any particular path by either her mother or her father.

"You are eager for my company, Lord Newton?" Georgina replied, seeing her mother's eyes flare at the slightly insolent tone which came through in Georgina's words. "But you are already in my company! Indeed, you have had my company every day this last sennight, save for Sunday, for you have called every day without fail!" She saw him nod eagerly but held up one hand. "Lord Newton, I am quite contented to save you a dance, but I will *not* guarantee that it will be the one you wish. The waltz is, as you know, the most intimate of dances and I should not like to dance it with a gentleman whom I know, in my heart, I would not truly consider, should he proceed to offer me any... *particular* attentions."

There was not an immediate response to this, as Georgina had hoped. Instead, Lord Newton simply looked back at her with a somewhat blank expression, as though he did not quite comprehend what she meant. Lady Kingham, however, slumped back in her chair, her eyes closing tightly as Georgina's words echoed about the room. Georgina waited, her mouth lifted in a small, half smile as a knot of tension began to form in her stomach. For whatever reason,

Lord Newton was either not taking in, or refusing to accept, what she was saying, and Georgina did not know what else she ought to do or say to make her opinion clear.

"Well," Lord Newton replied, after a few moments of utter silence, "if it is not to be the waltz, then I am quite content to settle for another dance." With a broad, beaming smile, he rose from his seat and bowed first to Lady Kingham – who had righted herself in her seat in a trice – and then to Georgina. Forced to rise, Georgina bade him farewell with as much courtesy as she could manage, although inwardly, her heart was sinking with both frustration and irritation. Lord Newton was either a little idiotic or he was being blatantly disrespectful in disregarding what she had said. Was he hoping that, somehow, she would be convinced to consider him when the time came for him to ask her to accept his suit?

"Georgina!"

The very moment that the door had closed behind Lord Newton, Lady Kingham was over by Georgina's side.

"Yes, mama?"

Georgina turned to look at her mother directly, with Lady Kingham only now a few steps away. By this time, all trace of calm propriety was gone from Lady Kingham, for her eyes were narrowed and glaring, with color rising in her cheeks. Georgina knew that she had upset her mother, but she could not feel even an ounce of regret, even though she had not managed to achieve what she had intended.

"It is just as well that Lord Newton is the forgiving sort, else you might have found yourself in particular difficulty, Georgina!" Lady Kingham reprimanded, shaking her finger in Georgina's direction. "How could you speak in such a way to Lord Newton? He is a gentleman!"

"And one who does not interest me in the least,"

Georgina retorted, firmly. "He has been very fervent in his calling upon me and, whilst I will not say I find his conversation *entirely* disagreeable, I *can* tell you that I find him both dull and inconsiderate." Her chin lifted as her mother opened her mouth to refute such a statement. "I am aware that he holds the title of Marquess, mama, but I will *not* consider him."

Lady Kingham's mouth closed, and she let out a long, pained sigh, her hands now clasping tightly together in front of her as though she could not bring herself to release them for fear that she might explode in anger. Georgina waited quietly, resisting the urge to say more, for fear of inducing her mother to greater fury. She knew that Lady Kingham did her best to make certain that Georgina met the highest titled unmarried gentlemen in London, but she did not seem to realize that their title was not something which Georgina considered. No matter how many times Georgina had attempted to explain, Lady Kingham had simply waved a hand and told her to stop being foolish. To her, title and fortune were all that was required to make a gentleman a suitable match for her daughter, whilst Georgina had the very opposite opinion.

"Georgina, there is nothing wrong with Lord Newton," Lady Kingham said, her voice very low and quiet, although Georgina knew that there was great restraint in her mother's words also. "You are refusing to consider him!"

"I *have* considered him, mama, and I find him disagreeable!" Georgina replied, throwing up her hands. "I care not that he is a Marquess, nor that he has an excellent fortune. He is too old for me and, besides which, shows no true consideration for either myself or you. In fact, his entire conversation and questions were centered solely on what he might gain for himself!" She drew in a breath, waiting to see if her mother would disagree, but Lady Kingham said nothing, merely dropping her head for a moment so that she might run one hand across her brow in a pained manner. "I do not think that I could ever be happy in Lord Newton's company," Georgina said, plainly. "I certainly could never see fit to wed him."

Lady Kingham let out a groan and fell back into her chair, leaving Georgina to ring the bell for refreshments. Given that Lord Newton had eaten all of their previous ones, she had no qualms in asking for another tray, regardless of what the staff might think of such a request.

"Then who are you to wed, Georgina?"

Georgina turned back from the bell to her mother, shrugging lightly as she did so. "I do not know, my dear Mama," she answered, quietly, "but it will not be Lord Newton, I can assure you of that!"

"Because you will not be pushed into accepting a gentleman that both your father and I think to be a suitable match!"

A slightly wry laugh escaped from Georgina's mouth and her mother turned to her sharply.

"Mama, both you and I know that father cares very little for my choices and considerations in this matter," she said, plainly. "Father is more concerned with his card games and business matters." She shrugged one shoulder. "His heir is wed and has already produced two very fine boys to continue the line. It is quite natural that he should not think much of my future."

Speaking carelessly, Georgina ignored the pain which lanced her heart at the truth of her words. Her father had never really cared for her and had always shown a great preference for his son. It was something of which she had always been aware but had come to accept, even if it did still bring her sorrow.

Lady Kingham tossed her head.

"Regardless of your father's considerations, you know very well that *I* have always done all I can for you, Georgina," she stated, firmly, refusing to be drawn on the matter of Lord Kingham. "Lord Newton is someone I consider to be more than suitable for you."

"Because he is a Marquess?" Georgina queried, her brow lifting. "Or is it because he displays such elegant manners, with his kind manner and generous character more than apparent?" The irony in her words did not escape Lady Kingham's notice, but Georgina was not yet finished. "I am tired of being paraded in front of the various gentlemen you consider suitable, only to be pulled away from any that I might wish to consider further!" she exclaimed, her irritation growing steadily. "The last gentleman I thought well of – Lord Burton – was refused by you and father when he asked to court me, simply because he was a Viscount!" Georgina had been upset by that particular decision, aware that it had been solely her mother's influence which had persuaded her father to refuse Lord Burton. "Should I not be permitted to make my own decision in such things, Mama?"

Lady Kingham drew herself up, her chin lifting as she looked back at her daughter.

"No," she said crisply, as Georgina's heart slammed hard in her chest. "You may not decide such things for yourself, Georgina. My mother guided me, and I have been very blessed indeed by her choice for me."

Georgina considered this and then shook her head.

"That may be so, Mama, but I am not of the same mind as you," she said, softly, not wanting to get into an argument with her mother but at the same time, doing all she could to make certain that her mother understood her point of view. "You may have thought it a delight to have your mother guide you into a suitable marriage, but I find that I am eager to make up my own mind about such matters. In fact, I would be both upset and frustrated to be forced into a marriage simply because *you* thought the gentleman a suitable match."

"You do not have any appreciation of my efforts nor my judgement!" Lady Kingham cried, throwing up her hands in exasperation. "Why do I have such an ungrateful daughter?"

A sharp retort sprang to Georgina's lips, but she forced them closed, refusing to say a single thing in response to her mother's question. It was not at all that she was unappreciative, nor that she did not want to hear her mother's opinion, but rather that she wanted simply to make up her own mind about something so important. To choose the gentleman whom she would be with for the rest of her days was something that Georgina did not want anyone but herself to decide.

"Lord Newton is worth your consideration, Georgina, and you *will* dance with him," Lady Kingham stated, her tone brooking no argument. "I am frustrated that you did not agree to save the waltz for him but, regardless, you will make certain that the dance is a suitable one and that Lord Newton is both satisfied and contented with your conduct and your conversation." Coming forward, she put one hand on Georgina's shoulder. Looking up, Georgina was surprised that there was no anger in her mother's eyes, nor even a flash of irritation in her expression. "I care for you very deeply, my dear," Lady Kingham said, speaking much more softly now. "I am doing all that I can to make certain that your future is a secure and settled one. The final decision will be yours, but I should like you to *try* to trust me, my dear, even a little bit."

Without saying anything more, Lady Kingham pressed Georgina's shoulder and then took her leave, walking from the room without even looking back at her daughter. Georgina followed her with her eyes, filled with such a confusion of feeling that it was all she could do not to call out after her mother. Once the door was closed, Georgina let out a long breath, sank back down into her chair, and put her head in her hands.

It was not, as her mother suspected, that she did not trust that her mother cared for her, nor that she did not want to listen to her judgment. It was merely that Georgina did not want the decision to be made for her. As much as Lady Kingham wanted Georgina to consider what *she* said, Georgina was just as eager for her mother to listen to Georgina's thoughts and opinions! But it was not to be, it seemed, for Lady Kingham appeared just as determined as ever to bring to the fore only the gentlemen that *she* considered to be suitable. And, given how much she was pressing Lord Newton forward – and doing so in spite of Georgina's objections – Georgina felt herself becoming both upset and frustrated. Her mother did not want to listen to what Georgina said and she was left with no other choice but to do as her mother had asked. Lord Newton would expect a dance tomorrow, and Georgina would have to grant it to him, even though she had no intention of considering him as a potential husband.

The final decision will be yours.

That, Georgina considered, was a blessing at least. Whilst her mother was content to allow Georgina to decide whether or not to accept the offer of marriage from any number of gentlemen who might wish to offer for her, Lady Kingham would make certain that only the gentlemen she thought suitable would ever be able to get to that point, in their connection with Georgina and her mother. It was a very difficult position for Georgina to be in at present and there appeared, unfortunately, to be very little she could do about it.

Blinking back a flurry of tears, Georgina lifted her head from her hands and tried to calm her upset. She did not want to think about the fact that, if she did not wed this Season then, with next Season being her third, her mother would become all the more desperate. No doubt she *would* find herself married to a gentleman she thought very little of and cared nothing for, for Lady Kingham would never permit Georgina to become a spinster.

"Then I must do something *this* Season," Georgina said aloud, trying to bolster her own confidence. "If I do not, then I will be relegated to that particular fate, and I will not allow that to happen!"

No immediate idea came to her, however. There was no instant recourse which flung itself into her mind, and nor did she catch her breath at the thought of any one particular gentleman who might satisfy both herself and her mother. Everything remained just as it was, save for a fresh burst of confidence that grew in Georgina's heart. Somehow, in some way, she would find an answer to the troubles that surrounded her at present. She might have to dance with Lord Newton, but Georgina was determined that she would not permit herself to be caught in such a way again. Regardless of her mother's own resolve, Georgina would carve her own path and make her own decisions about her future.

She was utterly determined.

CHAPTER TWO

Walking into the ballroom took more courage than Frederick had anticipated. It was not as though he had not been to a ball in London before, but it was just that he had not been to many. The first time he had walked into London society after having returned from the war, he had found himself being stared at and whispered about by seemingly almost everyone present! It had been a most discomfiting situation and, whilst Frederick had thrown it aside and told himself not to be ridiculous, he had not been able to pretend that he was not affected by it. The stares, and the ladies who clapped their hands to their mouths upon seeing him, had not filled him with confidence. Instead, it had only shaken his fortitude somewhat, even though, of course, he had not revealed the truth of his feelings to anyone.

He had been relieved at the time to have found an old friend in amongst the crowd, for Lord Ware had come to speak to him almost immediately, and had been absolutely delighted to see him. That had taken some of the strain from

Frederick's shoulders but, on this occasion, he felt very much alone.

I am here solely to make certain that I mingle in society and am acquainted with as many as I can be, he told himself, smiling broadly as he greeted his host for the evening. *How else am I to find those who side with the French if I do not know who is within London at present?*

"Good evening, Lord Stratham!" his host exclaimed, although Frederick noticed immediately how the gentleman's eyes went to his cheek. "I was so glad to hear that you were back in London."

Frederick forced his smile to remain in place, turning to speak to Lady Howard and to thank her for her kind invitation.

"I am enjoying my return to society," he replied, as Lady Howard rose from her curtsey. "Thank you for your invitation, it is wonderful to be here."

"Enjoy the evening!" Lord Howard exclaimed, slapping Frederick on the shoulder with a little more vigor than Frederick had expected. "It is so very good to see you again."

Frederick inclined his head and then made his way into the crowd, feeling the knot of tension still tight within his chest. He made sure to walk slowly, whilst keeping a small smile pinned to his lips so that no one would think him either melancholy or unhappy to be present. No one met his eye, no one stopped to greet him, and Frederick was left feeling even more uncertain of himself. His breath caught in his chest as he saw one lady looking at him, only for her eyes to widen before she turned away. Irritated at his foolish reaction, Frederick turned on his heel and made to go in search of the card room rather than remain here, only to be prevented by the presence of one particular gentleman.

Closing his eyes, Frederick let out a long breath of relief.

"Abernyte," he breathed, more than glad to see the Duke of Abernyte present. "You are returned."

The Duke chuckled as Frederick opened his eyes, his own eyes bright with evident enjoyment of the Ball. There were ladies on either side of him who, whilst not yet in conversation with the Duke, were clearly eager to step in at any moment.

"I am," Abernyte said, although there was a keenness in his expression which Frederick understood. "Bath was not as interesting as I believed it would be."

Frederick knew in an instant what the Duke referred to, aware that they could not speak openly at present. The Duke of Abernyte had gone to Bath with the expectation of finding out some particulars about the members of the *ton* who were eager to support the French. However, during the Duke's time in Bath, Frederick had discovered that the names they had been given had been nothing but a falsehood. He had been waiting for the Duke to return to London and now, it seemed, he had done so.

"I am sorry to hear that," he replied, as the Duke grinned, knowing that Frederick understood what was being expressed. "Perhaps you might find yourself more engaged here in London."

"I hope I shall!" came the reply. His eyes went to Frederick's cheek and then back to his eyes. "I was sorry to hear of your injury."

Shrugging, Frederick tried not to allow it to bother him.

"I would have preferred to remain in my role back with the army in the field, but circumstances have sent me here," he answered, quietly. "But there is still much to be done here in London. I have many responsibilities which will be a priority for me."

The Duke nodded, glancing to his right and his left before he drew a little closer, clearly wanting to speak now without being overheard.

"Might I call upon you tomorrow?" he asked, as Frederick nodded immediately. "There is much to discuss, and I only arrived back in London this afternoon, else I would have sent a note to you in advance."

"I would be very glad to see you," Frederick answered, honestly. "Lord Ware has..." Seeing one young lady move a little closer, Frederick shook his head, a wry smile on his lips. "Lord Ware has just taken leave of London to go on his wedding trip, but there are some things I am sure he wanted me to mention to you."

The Duke, noticing the young lady drawing closer, chuckled ruefully and stepped back.

"Certainly," he replied, as Frederick grinned, truly glad to see his friend again. "Now, would you like me to introduce you to any of my *lovely* acquaintances?" His eyes turned to his right and then to his left, gesturing to the ladies who were all still standing very close to him indeed. "I know that they would be glad to have someone new to converse with!"

Frederick shrugged, finding a slight wariness in his heart, but choosing to ignore it.

"If they would like to, then yes," Frederick replied, fearful that the scar on his face would turn some of them away from him. "Although I am not certain that many young ladies would like to speak or converse with..."

He lifted one hand towards his face, but the Duke only laughed.

"Allow *me* to introduce you and you will find yourself a

very eagerly sought after gentleman," he replied, one eyebrow lifting. "Come, come this way."

Frederick drew in a breath, forcing a smile and an air of confidence which he did not truly feel, before allowing the Duke to lead him to his right. Three young ladies stood together, their heads close to each other as they discussed the other attendees, the latest fashions, and society news. An older lady behind them nudged one of them and, in an instant, all three young ladies had lifted their heads, stopped their conversation, and turned to face them.

Waiting for the Duke to introduce him to these three young women, Frederick saw the first, then the second, and then the third all turn to glance at him, their eyes each lingering on the mark on his face. His stomach dropped to the floor. This was not going to be as easy as the Duke had anticipated, he was sure of it.

"Might I introduce a dear friend of mine?" the Duke of Abernyte boomed, his voice seeming to carry halfway across the ballroom. "This is the Marquess of Stratham." He placed one hand on Frederick's shoulder as Frederick bowed low, not quite certain what the Duke intended to say next. "Lord Stratham has been one of the most important gentlemen in the war effort," the Duke continued, now slapping Frederick gently on the back. "He has come up with strategies, organized the militia, and, on many an occasion, made certain that *I* was kept from danger." His brow furrowed as the three young ladies gasped. "It is known to the *ton* that I was a little involved in the war, but what is not known is the duty which Lord Stratham paid to me. Through his advice, his knowledge, and his general wisdom, not only I but a good many other men were kept safe."

He threw an admiring glance towards Frederick, who found himself flushing with embarrassment. It was not *exactly* as the Duke had said it, but there was still an appreciation in Frederick's heart for what the Duke was attempting to do. The man was trying to lift Frederick up in the eyes of the young ladies so that they might see his injury as a reflection of the work he had done for King and country, rather than something which would be otherwise objectionable.

"You speak much too grandly of me, Your Grace," Frederick replied, seeing the gleam in the Duke's eye. "But I thank you."

"Not at all," the Duke replied, gesturing to the three young ladies. "Might I then introduce Miss Yarrow, Lady Matilda, and Lady Florence."

Frederick bowed again and the three young ladies curtsied. However, when they rose, there was no longer a flicker of uncertainty in their gaze. Instead, there was an interest in their expression which Frederick could not mistake for anything other than blatant curiosity. A small swirl of warmth rose in his heart as he looked back at the three young ladies. Perhaps the Duke of Abernyte's return would be even better than Frederick had anticipated.

"Good to see you, Abernyte."

Frederick walked across the room, his hand held out so that he might shake the Duke's hand firmly. He spoke with an easy familiarity that came with being long friends with such a gentleman, to the point that he did not have to speak so deferentially. War had a way of removing all such rank, all such superiority between gentlemen. A pauper and a Duke might fight together and find themselves not only friends but comrades. It did not matter whether or not they were separated by rank; in war, they were brothers.

"You enjoyed yourself last evening, then?"

Frederick chuckled, a broad smile pulling at his lips.

"You know very well that I did," he answered, as the Duke grinned, making his way across the room so that he might sit down. "After your influence, those three young ladies seemed more than eager to become all the better acquainted with me!" He had not danced with any others save for those three, but Frederick considered that to be an excellent foray into returning fully into society. Hopefully, those three young ladies would speak of him to their friends and acquaintances, and, in time, others would not look at him with such aversion.

"I am glad that I was able to assist," the Duke murmured, looking at Frederick with some concern in his eyes. "Are you quite well, my friend?"

Frederick nodded.

"Very well," he answered, honestly. "In truth, Abernyte, I did not want to leave the field. I did not want to return, but it was taken out of my hands." His lips flattened for a moment. "However, there is something here that I can do, at least."

The Duke nodded gravely.

"Indeed there is," he answered, all mirth gone from his expression. "I have heard that the names we were given were not genuine."

"And thus, your trip to Bath was not at all merited and, in fact, a waste of time," Frederick replied, walking to the corner of the room so that he might pour them both a small whisky. "But there is news." Briefly, he told the Duke of Abernyte all that had transpired recently with Lord Ware and his two acquaintances. "We have them both, of course, and there will be consequences for their treason, but their capture is being kept far from society's ears, for fear that any others involved in the matter will become wary."

The Duke frowned.

"But they will note their absence."

"Of course," Frederick agreed, "but there will be no knowledge of *why* they have disappeared from London, and certainly, they will have no awareness as to which of us within society are seeking them out."

Slowly, a look of understanding spread across the Duke's face.

"I see." His lips quirked. "No doubt you have your particular set of servants ready to do as you ask them?"

Frederick chuckled, knowing exactly what the Duke referred to. Since he had returned to London, Frederick had made certain to hire a small group of men who had both the strength of mind and of body to aid him whenever it was required. It had been a wise decision to do so, for they had already proved themselves invaluable.

"So what are we to do now?" the Duke asked, swirling his whisky for a few moments. "Lord Ware is on his wedding trip, did you not say? He cannot be of aid at present."

"Yes, that is correct," Frederick confirmed. "But he has written recently. The invasion we feared is still being planned by our enemy, it seems. They intend to move very soon, by summer."

A long, frustrated breath escaped from the Duke's lips.

"But they still will not reveal themselves to us easily. And as such, we have very little certainty as to who we might even think to consider!"

"Not so," Frederick replied, quickly. "Lord Ware, before he married, had discovered that there was a small gathering of those who were eager to support the French. He intended to join it under the guise of being sympathetic to them, but his plans were thwarted. Nevertheless, the meeting will be taking place very soon, and we *must* find a way to infiltrate it."

The Duke nodded slowly, one hand running over his chin for a few moments as he considered all that Frederick had told him.

"There was one name which has been mentioned to me," he said, slowly. "You will recall that when I was at the coast – when I was absent for some time due to the illness which now believe was an attempt to poison me – there were some who were captured and taken prisoner due to their ill deeds."

"I did not know of it at the time, but you did write to inform me, yes," Frederick replied, slowly. "I do not remember all that you detailed but–"

"The fellow who had attempted to poison me spoke of various things," the Duke continued, waving a hand as an apology for interrupting Frederick. "He did mention, on two separate occasions, that a gentleman in London had been of assistance, although not involved in anything specific."

Frederick lifted an eyebrow.

"Oh?"

"'Lord K'," the Duke answered, helpfully. "Not a specific name and, at the time, I disregarded it simply because there was so much else to consider, but perhaps that might give us something to aim for."

His spirits lifted and Frederick agreed quickly. Rather than fumbling around vaguely in the dark, they now had something specific to work towards.

"Something to consider, certainly," he replied, as the

Duke threw back the rest of his whisky. "Although there are a few gentlemen who have a title beginning with a 'K'."

The Duke shrugged.

"There are, but we need to acquaint ourselves with all of them. In addition, I have had news that Lord Brinsworth is returning to England."

Frederick frowned.

"Lord Brinsworth?"

"He will be a helpful addition," the Duke continued, clearly acquainted with the gentleman whilst Frederick struggled to recall whether or not he knew the name. "He is as you are – not at all inclined towards remaining here in London and wanting very much to return to the war, but he will not be able to at present."

Frederick did not ask more but his fingers absent-mindedly traced the scar on his cheek, feeling that heavy weight that came whenever he thought about how he had been refused his request to remain with the army.

"He requires a little more time to recover – he is at his estate at present – but I believe that he has intentions of returning to London for at least part of the Season." A wry smile pulled at his mouth. "His mother is eager to do so, and I fear that being a good son and honorable gentleman, he will have very little choice!"

Laughing, Frederick took a sip of whisky and let the warmth flood his chest.

"Indeed. Well then, I shall be glad to have him here."

"More than he will be glad to be present, no doubt," the Duke warned. "Well then, all that is required now is for us to continue to make our way through society and to do all we can to make certain that we acquaint ourselves with every 'Lord K' that we know!"

A rueful smile tipped Frederick's lips.

"I can think of at least three already," he replied. "I am sure that there will be at least three others."

Laughing, the Duke threw back his head for a few moments.

"Ah, but some of them are bound to have daughters!" he exclaimed, holding out his glass for another measure of whisky. "And that is surely the easiest way for us to become acquainted with each and every gentleman!"

"Mayhap for you, certainly," Frederick replied, pouring whisky into both empty glasses. "Had it not been for you last evening, I am certain that most of the *ton* would have ignored my company and would, instead, have simply stared at me." He shook his head. "It has been that way ever since I returned to London and I fear will continue to be so, unless, of course, I am in *your* company."

"Nonsense!" the Duke cried, holding up his glass as though he were toasting Frederick. "Only a few words about the war and your involvement in it and they will not even notice the mark! They will want nothing more than to be in your company *and* in your arms... dancing, I mean." He chuckled, his eyes gleaming. "Trust me, Stratham. It will be just as I say, I have no doubt about it."

CHAPTER THREE

"*W*hether you wish it or not, you *will* dance with him!"

Lady Kingham's voice was filled with anger, but Georgina lifted her chin, her eyes blazing with fire.

"I will *not!*" she exclaimed, her hands planted firmly on her hips. "And you will not be able to persuade me to do so, Mama. Just because he is a gentleman with a high title and great fortune does not mean that he is in any way suitable!" She recoiled at the idea of standing up with a gentleman who had, when he had last called, not so much as glanced at Georgina's face but had, instead, talked only of himself and allowed his gaze to pour down Georgina's figure without any hesitation whatsoever. "Lord Jeffries is *not* a gentleman I consider to be a suitable match."

"But *I* do," her mother proclaimed, coming towards Georgina. "You *will* dance with him, should he ask, else I will... I will..."

Georgina's smile was triumphant. There was nothing her mother could threaten which would force Georgina to act as she wished. After all, there was naught that Lady

Kingham could do which would prevent Georgina from making her own decisions. She could threaten to take Georgina from society, to force her to remain at home, but all she would be doing in that particular regard was preventing her daughter from being seen by society and furthering her acquaintance – which was Lady Kingham's goal.

"I will make certain that you will wed Lord Newton!"

Georgina caught her breath, her eyes widening as she stared at her mother. All sense of victory faded from her as she looked into Lady Kingham's face and saw the seriousness which now filled her expression.

"You cannot be serious, Mama!" Georgina exclaimed, horror flooding her. "You have always said that I can make my own decision as regards my marriage, and I have clung to that promise!"

"But such a promise is making you behave in this ridiculous, unruly manner!" Lady Kingham stated, her shoulders dropping as though she had now settled herself entirely. "There has to be something that I can do to make you behave as you ought. Therefore, if I choose to rescind that agreement, then I will do so."

There was no immediate reply, no instant retort which flung itself to Georgina's lips. Her heart was thumping furiously, her anger and upset tying themselves together. She could not have her mother dictate such a thing and, given the last few weeks, Georgina had believed that it would never occur. However, now it seemed that her mother had decided to change her mind entirely, leaving Georgina facing a very unfavorable future.

"No!"

"Now," Lady Kingham said, softly, ignoring Georgina's explosion of horror, "should Lord Jeffries ask you to dance with him this evening, whether it be one dance or two, you will accept him with all gratitude and even delight!" She came closer to Georgina, putting one hand on her arm as if to comfort her. "I am not stating outright that I will force you to wed any particular gentleman, Georgina. But I *must* have you behaving correctly and stop this attempt at insolence!" Her eyes sparked with anger, and Georgina suddenly realized just how upset her mother truly was. A wave of shame came over her and she dropped her head. "Do you understand me, Georgina?"

Georgina nodded, choosing not to answer aloud.

There was a great mix of emotions within her, and she could not quite make sense of all that she felt. There was a sense of shame about how poorly she had been behaving in refusing outright to do as her mother asked, yet there was also that determination to make her own decisions. She could not permit herself to be forced into matrimony with any gentleman she did not like and, at the same time, found herself desperately bored with all that her mother forced her to do. Were she permitted to acquaint herself further with a gentleman – *any* gentleman that she was interested in – then perhaps she would find it easier to deal with her mother's expectations.

There was no time for Georgina to discuss things further with Lady Kingham for her mother was, by this time, already making her way from the room. Georgina swallowed hard, drew in and let out a long breath, and then, finally, followed after her. For this evening at least, she would have to do as her mother asked but, thereafter, she would have to think of a solution, a manner in which she might escape her mother's demands.

"Good evening, Lady Georgina."

Georgina let out a breath of relief and quickly slipped one hand through her friend, Lady Matilda's, arm.

"I am *very* glad to see you," she murmured, as Lady Matilda let out a giggle of surprise at Georgina's fervor. She searched Lady Matilda's face. "Pray, is there any news of your brother?"

Matilda's face clouded immediately.

"No, there is not," she answered, her smile breaking apart as she looked back at Georgina. "My uncle remains stoic, but mother is insistent that we do *something*."

Georgina frowned. Lady Matilda's father, Lord Kellingston, had died some years ago and, since then, both Lady Matilda and her mother had relied heavily on Lord Hampton, Lady Kellingston's brother. At the time of Lord Kellingston's death, Lady Matilda's brother had been in France, fighting. When letters had been sent to tell him that he was now Lord Kellingston, the troubling news had come back that he was missing. Lord Hampton had been doing all he could to find news of the missing Lord Kellingston but, thus far, there had been nothing.

"But what could be done?" she asked, knowing that Lady Matilda's brother had most likely been captured by the French as he fought for King and country and held far from London if he had not already been killed. "Has your uncle no influence?"

Lady Matilda shrugged and tossed her head, letting out a long breath.

"I do not know the particulars," she replied, a little more briskly, "but I do not want to speak of him this evening. I already have too much moroseness from Mama, so I must enjoy this evening whilst I can!" She smiled, brightness coming back into her expression. "Tell me, why were you so very glad to see me?"

Georgina cast a glance towards her mother.

"Come," she murmured, doing as Lady Matilda had asked and set all thought of her brother aside. "My mother will not mind if we take a short turn about the room, so long as we stay near to her." Catching her mother's eye, Georgina gestured to Lady Matilda. After a few moments, Lady Kingham gave her a small nod of consent and Georgina let out a long breath of relief. "I have so much that I need to speak with you about."

Lady Matilda looked at her with concern.

"Whatever is the matter?"

"My mother insists that I do as she says, else she will force me to marry Lord Newton," she told her friend, hearing Lady Matilda's gasp of horror. "But any gentleman whom I consider, my mother will not even *think* of listening to my thoughts about, for she is quite determined that she knows what is best." Sighing heavily, Georgina patted Lady Matilda's hand. "Do you have any advice as to what I might do?"

Lady Matilda shrugged.

"Find a gentleman whom you consider to be suitable *and* that your mother could not disagree with," she stated, as though it would be the easiest thing in the world for Georgina to achieve. "There must be someone here that she would think agreeable." Her eyes brightened. "The Duke of Abernyte is now returned to London! Why not consider him?"

Georgina laughed, her eyes twinkling.

"And I must pry him away from every other young lady in all of London, must I not?" Lady Matilda laughed as Georgina continued. "I will have to bat my eyelashes, smile demurely, and do all that I can to make certain that the Duke thinks of no one but me."

"I am certain that you can do it, should you decide to," Lady Matilda replied, her confidence making Georgina smile. "He would make an excellent husband, I am sure."

This remark made Georgina shake her head.

"I could not say that for certain, Matilda," she replied, a small frown catching her brow. "Just because a gentleman has an excellent title – even a title only a little less than a Prince – does not mean that he has a good character."

"Oh, but the *ton* all say so," Lady Matilda replied, with a confidence that Georgina could not quite agree with. "Come, I will introduce him to you if you wish it? I have been introduced already."

Georgina's frown deepened.

"Have you?" she asked, seeing Lady Matilda's bright smile. "Then I suppose that there is nothing wrong with being introduced to a Duke!" Her frown lifted. "Even if he is entirely disagreeable, it would please my mother."

"Then we shall do so at once!" Lady Matilda exclaimed, turning swiftly so that she might lead Georgina back towards their respective mothers. "Come, let us ask my mother to accompany us to him."

LADY KINGHAM's agreement was instantaneous and, together, the four made their way across the room to find the Duke of Abernyte. He was not difficult to find. There was a great crowd of guests, yes, but they were mostly congregated in one corner of the room and Georgina was quite certain that this was where the Duke now stood. Lady Matilda was discussing many things about the Duke's character with both Georgina and Lady Kingham, but Georgina was not truly listening. Instead, she simply walked quietly alongside her mother, feeling a small knot of anticipation and excitement tie itself in her stomach. Could the Duke be the gentleman that she had been looking for? A gentleman who might be of excellent character *and* hold a title that would satisfy her mother?

"Oh, my goodness!"

Lady Matilda came to a stop as she saw the crowd of people who now surrounded the Duke of Abernyte. Georgina could only see a glimpse of him but the little she did see told her that he was very handsome indeed. Her excitement faded away, however, as she realized just how difficult it would be to even find herself introduced to him! The Duke's return to London had clearly been highly anticipated and Georgina did not think that she would ever be able to find herself solely in his company!

"I – I think we should wait for a few moments," Georgina said, as her mother let out a long, heavy sigh. "There are far too many people near him, and we cannot simply push our way through."

"It is to be expected, given his title and absence from London of late," Lady Kellingston stated, although Georgina did not miss the pride which flashed through her expression. She was quite delighted that she and Lady Matilda had already been introduced to the Duke of Abernyte, whilst Georgina knew that her mother would be more than disappointed that, as yet, she had not been.

"How disheartening," Lady Kingham replied, softly. "But you are quite right to state that it is to be expected. The Duke of Abernyte is a *very* popular gentleman and I must admit that even I am delighted to know that he is returned to London!" Her eyes flicked to Georgina. "It would be good to be introduced to him, however, Georgina. Mayhap you should attempt to be so this evening, in one way or another."

Georgina's lips curved in a half-smile.

"But I would not wish to miss any of my dances, Mama," she answered, as her mother frowned. "Especially if Lord Jeffries is to seek me out to dance with me."

"Lord Jeffries?" Lady Kellingston glanced first at Georgina and then at Lady Kingham. "My dear friend, not that it is my place to state my opinion of a gentleman outright, but I do not think too highly of Lord Jeffries." She shook her head. "He may appear to be quite gentlemanly, and his title is certainly an excellent one, but I have heard that his character is severely lacking."

Georgina's brows rose, but Lady Kingham said nothing. In fact, Lady Kellingston's remarks seemed only to cause her mother's frown to deepen. Georgina sent a grateful smile towards Lady Kellingston, who returned it with one of her own.

As Georgina looked back towards the Duke, her attention was caught suddenly by another gentleman. He stood nearby, watching the Duke with a small smile on his face. It was not his expression that Georgina noticed, however, but rather the scar which ran down one side of his face. It was long and quite red, making her wonder if it was a recent injury. How had he come about it? And was he acquainted with the Duke already?

"The gentleman you are observing is the Marquess of Stratham," Lady Matilda said, interrupting Georgina's thoughts. "I was introduced to him at the last Ball, by the Duke himself!"

"Indeed," Georgina murmured, continuing to look at

the gentleman and not lifting her gaze from him. "A Marquess, did you say?"

Lady Kingham put one hand on Georgina's shoulder.

"You cannot consider him, Georgina," she said, firmly. "Not when he has such a... a *mark!*"

"It came from the war," Lady Matilda replied, looking at Lady Kingham with a shrewd glance, her lips flattening as though she disliked Lady Kingham's tone just as much as Georgina did. "He was injured with both a bayonet *and* a sword, although it is impossible to say which one did *that.*" She glanced at Georgina. "A fall from his horse during the battle added to his injuries and sent him back to London – although I do believe that, during their time fighting together, Lord Stratham was of great help to the Duke of Abernyte – at least, that is what the Duke said."

This did not seem to soften Lady Kingham's impression of the gentleman, however, for her expression remained a little blank, and not even a spark of interest came into her eyes. Georgina, however, found herself feeling quite the opposite. Her interest was piqued, her eagerness to find out more about the gentleman growing steadily. He was different from other gentlemen, certainly, and Georgina had to admit that she thought him very courageous indeed. Not every member of the *ton* would have the boldness to step out into society with such an injury for, without any doubt, news of his scar would have spread all through London at great speed. And there would be many who would drop him lower in their estimation than he deserved... her mother included. Her lips twisted as she scowled. It was frustrating indeed that an outward flaw, any minute imperfection, would be seen and judged by the *ton* and she had no doubt that Lord Stratham was now deemed to be a little less suitable by the many mothers who chaperoned their daughters through society.

But he is a Marquess, at least.

Georgina's lips lifted as she turned her gaze to her mother.

"But he is a Marquess, Mama," Georgina said, softly. "You wanted me to consider a gentleman with a higher title than my father's, did you not?" She threw out one hand towards Lord Stratham. "There is a Marquess!" She grasped Lady Matilda's hand. "Lady Matilda, might you be willing to introduce me?"

"Georgina!"

Lady Kingham's hand tightened on Georgina's shoulder.

"Lady Matilda?" Georgina said again, seeing how her friend glanced first at Lady Kingham and then back to Georgina herself. She widened her eyes and gave a tiny nod in her friend's direction, asking her silently to do as she asked, even though Lady Kingham was less than willing. Lady Matilda hesitated, looked towards Lord Stratham, and then grinned.

"But of course!" she exclaimed, proving to Georgina once more just how similar they were in terms of their determination and their considerations. "Have no doubt, Lady Kingham, we will remain in your sight throughout."

Relieved, Georgina stepped away from her mother before she could protest further, looping her arm through Lady Matilda's once more.

"Thank you," she murmured, as her friend laughed softly. "My mother thinks him less than worthy simply due to how he looks, I am sure of it."

Lady Matilda pressed her arm.

"But you do not."

"No," Georgina replied, firmly, her gaze now fixed to Lord Stratham. "*I* do not."

She smiled as she saw Lord Stratham glance towards them, his brow furrowing just a little as though he could not quite believe that they were coming to speak to him. Lady Matilda cleared her throat gently, dropping into a quick curtsey as Lord Stratham turned a little more towards them.

"Good evening, Lord Stratham!" Lady Matilda exclaimed, as the gentleman bowed. "I do hope that you are having a pleasant evening?"

Georgina used these few minutes, as Lady Matilda spoke, to take Lord Stratham in. She did not look at his injury but rather at his eyes, seeing the uncertainty which lingered in his expression and finding herself feeling rather sympathetic towards him. No doubt, he was expecting her either to stare at his scar or to turn away from him with a mixture of disgust and horror. She did neither, however. Instead, she found herself quite taken with the color of his eyes, for they were neither brown nor green but seemed to be either one or both at once, depending on which way he looked. Georgina found herself thinking him quite handsome, seeing how the candlelight set his fair hair into a burnished bronze. Her lips curved gently and, as she looked back into his eyes, Georgina saw the surprise which now lingered there. It was as though he had never expected her to consider him in such a fashion, as though he could tell that her smile was not one of mocking, but of genuine interest. Such was his surprise that she thought, he was now quite uncertain as to how to behave.

"Lord Stratham?"

Lady Matilda spoke again, a little uncertainty in her voice as she waited for Lord Stratham to respond. Clearing his throat, Lord Stratham pulled his gaze from Georgina and then placed a smile on his lips.

"Forgive me, Lady Matilda. I am very much enjoying the evening, yes," he replied, although Georgina was certain that he did not speak the whole truth, given how others in society must regard him. "I have been waiting to speak to the Duke of Abernyte, but I do not think that such a thing will take place any time soon!"

Lady Matilda laughed, her eyes twinkling.

"Indeed, I should think not," she replied, as Georgina threw a glance back towards the gentleman, seeing how he was still practically surrounded by young ladies and their respective mothers. "Given that you will be unable to speak to the Duke of Abernyte at present, might I perhaps introduce a friend of mine to you?" She turned to Georgina who quickly smiled as warmly as she could. "Lord Stratham, this is Lady Georgina Fielding, daughter to the Earl of Kingham."

Georgina dropped into a curtsey but not before she had noticed the interest which suddenly sprang into Lord Stratham's eyes. She could not explain it – unless it was that he now considered her a suitable match given that he now knew her position within society. Her stomach lurched as she rose from her curtsey, her smile now a little fixed. To have such consideration was no consideration at all.

"Lady Georgina," Lord Stratham murmured, bowing. "I am delighted to make your acquaintance."

"As I am in making yours, Lord Stratham," Georgina replied, now a little uncertain of him. "You say you have been enjoying the evening? Have you been in London for long?"

He smiled at her, his eyes now seeming to glow just a little.

"Not for a good length of time, no," he replied, quietly. "But I have returned and, as such, London society will have to simply become used to such a fellow being in their midst!"

Georgina knew full well what he referred to, but chose not to continue the conversation in that direction, not wanting to talk about his scar nor ask any questions about it. She wanted, for whatever reason, to be quite different from the rest of the *ton*. If Lord Stratham wished to explain what had occurred, then he would tell her when he was ready to do so. She, for her own sake as well as for his, would show no interest whatsoever.

"And are you to dance this evening, Lord Stratham?" she asked, tilting her head slightly. "I have not yet seen you standing up with anyone."

A slight flush came into his cheeks.

"I am to dance, yes," he answered, his words now a little strained. "But as yet, I have not found a suitable partner." His brow furrowed and he glanced first at Georgina and then to Lady Matilda. "If you would be so kind as to permit me, I should be glad to take one of your dances, Lady Matilda?"

Georgina felt a flush of heat creep up her face as she waited for Lady Matilda to hand her dance card to Lord Stratham. Had she truly been expecting Lord Stratham to ask her first? And if that was the case *why* had she thought such a thing? That was naught but arrogance and Georgina was ashamed of herself for thinking such a thing. Patiently, she waited until Lord Stratham turned to her, as she knew he would.

"Lady Georgina?" he asked, his tone a little softer. "Might you honor me also?"

Out of the corner of her eye, Georgina saw something

move. Glancing away from Lord Stratham, she saw her mother standing nearby, having lifted her hand to catch Georgina's attention. Georgina did not doubt that her mother would firmly disapprove of Georgina's dancing with Lord Stratham, but she did not care. Seeing how Lady Kingham frowned, how her eyes narrowed, Georgina lifted her chin and turned back to Lord Stratham, seeing the flicker of worry in his eyes.

"Certainly, Lord Stratham," she said, with as much warmth as possible. "I would be *very* glad to dance with you."

And so saying, she handed him her dance card with a broad smile and a sense of triumph in her heart. Her mother would not win when it came to this particular gentleman, nor this matter. She would dance with whom she wished and, whilst her mother might insist on her stepping out with Lord Jeffries, Georgina would not be held back from other gentlemen who might ask her. With a deep breath, Georgina settled her shoulders and held her head high, ignoring the furious glare which came from her mother's direction. She was already looking forward to her dance.

CHAPTER FOUR

"*I* have finally found you alone."

Frederick grinned as the Duke of Abernyte rolled his eyes, although he was quite certain that his friend very much enjoyed the company of others.

"It is a rare thing, indeed," the Duke sighed, as though such a thing was a great burden. "I should very much like to be left alone, but they simply will not permit me to be so!"

"How difficult a trial that must be for you," Frederick replied, sarcasm ringing through his tone. "How much you must wish to be in *my* position, where I am ignored entirely by the majority of the *ton*!" He had not meant to sound bitter but, as he finished speaking, Frederick was all too aware of that particular sound being in his tone. Giving himself a slight shake, he cleared his throat and shrugged. "Forgive me."

The Duke settled one hand on Frederick's shoulder for a moment.

"Not at all, old boy," he replied, in a voice which told Frederick that his friend sympathized greatly. "It is quite understandable for you to feel so. I am sorry that the *ton* treats you as they do, although I must continue to hope that not all of them are so inclined?"

He lifted one eyebrow and Frederick nodded quickly, shaking away the rest of his lingering melancholy.

"Not all, no," he said, swiftly. "I have been a little irritated with some of the looks which are thrown in my direction, but aside from that, I have made one new acquaintance and have even found myself ready to dance with one or two!" He saw the Duke's brows lift and let out a small laugh. "Indeed, I was just as surprised as you, but it is quite so." Leaning a little closer, he spoke in a quieter tone. "And one, Lady Georgina Fielding, is the daughter of the Earl of Kingham." The Duke's brows rose even higher, and Frederick felt a sense of satisfaction fill him. "Indeed, it is quite so," he said, as the Duke began to nod slowly. "And quite by chance!" He shrugged one shoulder. "Not that I am stating that the young lady *or* her father are at all involved in this affair as regards the French, but we are to look for a 'Lord K' are we not?"

"We are," the Duke replied, now looking quite pleased. "Very well done there, Stratham! And you secured a dance with the lady, you say?" Seeing Frederick nod, the Duke rubbed his chin for a few moments, his gaze going across the ballroom. "You have every reason to call on her thereafter, then."

"I do," Frederick agreed, knowing that such a thing would be expected regardless, although it would also allow him to perhaps be introduced to the Earl of Kingham himself. "I have not yet been introduced to Lady Kingham, although I presume that she is present this evening."

The Duke of Abernyte chuckled, his eyes twinkling.

"That would be a wise endeavor, then," he replied,

"although I confess that the thought of being introduced to any young lady's mother often fills me with dread."

"I can imagine," Frederick replied, dryly. "For they must be all quite delighted with you. They will be less delighted with me."

"Either reaction is a difficult one," the Duke answered, his lips still pulled into a grin. "But yes, a capital opportunity, Stratham!"

Frederick did not reply, for his attention had been caught by Lady Georgina, seeing her step out to dance with another gentleman. Her expression was quite different from when she had been conversing with him. There was no smile upon it and even her eyes appeared quite set. There was a hardness there that surely even her dance partner could not mistake, and Frederick was quite certain that the lady, at that present moment, had no wish to dance.

"Might I presume that this is the lovely Lady Georgina?"

The Duke's voice seemed to come from far away and it took Frederick a few moments to respond. Clearing his throat, he nodded but found himself quite unable to take his eyes away from the lady.

"Yes," he replied, a trifle briskly to hide from the Duke – and perhaps even from himself – just how interested he had been in watching the lady. "An excellent opportunity, as you said," he murmured.

The Duke nodded and moved a step closer, as though he wished to study the lady with a little more care. Frederick permitted his gaze to linger on her, recalling how she had watched him with evident interest rather than any obvious sign of displeasure or dislike. He had been expecting it, had been waiting for her face to change, for her lips to purse or her eyes to fall to the ground as her cheeks

paled. Instead, she had simply smiled at him – and it had
been a smile of warmth rather than of pity. Frederick had
not known what to make of her, for ever since his return to
London, he had not been treated with anything like that
amount of kind interest.

The Lady was, of course, quite lovely. Almost all young
ladies present during the Season were, of course, given that
they were decked out in their finery and had been under the
scrutiny of their respective mothers for some time before
making their come out! However, Lady Georgina was, he
considered, a little more fine than most. Her dark hair had
been pulled back tightly, allowing him full view of her fine
cheekbones and oval face. Her lips were full, her cheeks a
gentle pink but her large blue eyes, framed by dark lashes,
had been what had caught his attention the most. They
were almost violet, he had thought, but there was a spark
within them which had spoken of tenacity and vigor. Nor
had Frederick missed the way that Lady Georgina had
thrown a glance to her left as he had asked for her dance
card. It had not been until after he had returned it to her
that he had permitted himself to glance towards the lady in
question and had seen her dark frown and thin, pursed lips.
He presumed that this was none other than Lady Kingham
and that she disliked the fact that her daughter had handed
Frederick her dance card. No doubt it was due to his scar,
and, for a few moments, the awareness had unsettled him.
But then had come a sense of gladness that Lady Georgina,
at least, had not permitted herself to be overcome by his
changed face and had, instead, accepted his offer of a dance
without hesitation.

He did not think that Lady Kingham would be glad to
acquaint herself with him, however, although Frederick
knew that it would have to be done. One could not dance

with a young lady without being acquainted – either before or soon thereafter – with their mother or chaperone!

"I do not think that Lady Georgina is at all delighted to be standing up with Lord Jeffries," the Duke remarked, bringing Frederick out of his own considerations. "Her expression is almost morose!"

Frederick, seeing how the lady now appeared, let out a wry chuckle.

"I do not think that I can blame her for her lack of willingness, however," he said, as the Duke grinned. "Lord Jeffries is not the best of dancers."

"Nor the best of gentlemen," the Duke added, shaking his head. "Ah now, you must permit me to excuse myself, Stratham." He turned towards Frederick, although his eyes were fixed on someone behind. "The next dance will soon take place and I am to stand up with Miss Fairfax. Do excuse me."

Throwing a glance over his shoulder and seeing a fair-haired, rosy-cheeked young lady batting her eyelashes at the Duke, Frederick let out a chuckle, slapping the Duke on the shoulder before he stepped away. The Duke was not without company, and he could have his pick of young ladies to dance with – and it was clear that he was choosing the very prettiest of young ladies. It was not as though either Frederick or the Duke had any intention of marrying, but the *ton* were not aware of that and thus, they would continue, no doubt, to push their young ladies towards the Duke of Abernyte as much as possible.

"Do excuse me, Lord Stratham."

Frederick turned back swiftly, looking into the eyes of one Lady Kellingston, whom he had been introduced to some days ago. He could still see the flicker of revulsion in her eyes, although she wore a fixed smile that did not reach any other part of her expression.

"Good evening, Lady Kellingston!" he replied, relieved that he had recalled the lady's name. "How very good to see you again." He bowed low. "I have just had the pleasure of writing my name on your daughter's dance card." Lady Kellingston's smile grew but she still did not speak. "I was also grateful for her introduction to another of her friends," Frederick added quickly, wondering if Lady Kellingston was looking for a way to speak of such a thing without being too apparent. "A Lady Georgina Fielding."

"Yes, Lady Georgina!" Lady Kellingston exclaimed, stepping to one side swiftly and allowing another lady to move forward. "This, Lord Stratham, is the Countess of Kingham." She hesitated, then spread her hands. "Lady Georgina's mother." Gesturing toward Frederick, she then looked back at her friend. "Lady Kingham, the Marquess of Stratham."

Frederick bowed quickly, making sure to deliver a deep bow in the hope that this would somehow make Lady Kingham think well of him.

"Lady Kingham," he replied, rising slowly. "I am glad to make your acquaintance. I had hoped to do so this evening, given that I am already acquainted with your lovely daughter."

Lady Kingham's expression did not change. Instead, she continued to study him with narrowed eyes, and a scowl on her face as she looked boldly at his scar, her lip lifting in evident disgust.

Frederick placed his hands behind his back and clasped them together tightly, allowing some of the anger he felt at her reaction to go into them, helping him to keep his composure. He forced a smile and looked back at Lady Kingham steadily, not shrinking away from her as if he had something to hide. Lady Kingham's eyes were as blue as her daughter's but held none of the warmth, none of the kindness. There was, however, the same determination in her face which Frederick had seen in Lady Georgina's. Lady Kingham was a lady to be reckoned with.

"My daughter came to acquaint herself with you despite my urgings that she do no such thing, Lord Stratham," she said, eventually. Her voice was high-pitched and held no warmth whatsoever. "I did not wish her to do so. It was clear that she—"

"She was to be introduced to the Duke of Abernyte, you understand," Lady Kellingston interrupted, taking some of the sting from her friend's words. "It was only when we drew closer to him that we realized just how... sought after he is."

Frederick allowed a wry smile to touch his lips.

"Indeed, I quite understand," he answered, turning again towards Lady Kingham, and looking back into her face without hesitation. Despite his own uncertainty and confusion as regarded the lady, he did not want to allow Lady Kingham to think that he could be so easily insulted. "I am sorry that you did not wish it, Lady Kingham. Was there a reason for such a feeling?"

He lifted his chin a notch and lifted his chin, as though daring her to answer his question honestly.

To her credit, Lady Kingham did not answer as he expected her to. Instead, she turned her head away, looking a trifle abashed as her eyes met those of Lady Kellingston. Mayhap she had not expected him to answer in such a manner, or perhaps she had thought that he would be embarrassed by her directness. Or, mayhap she had expected him to know precisely *why* she had not wanted her daughter to dance with him and therefore, believed that he would not have needed to ask her such a thing. Frederick kept his eyes locked to Lady Kingham, waiting until she looked back at him and then, carefully and deliberately, arching one eyebrow in question.

"I – I merely thought that it was improper for her to do so given that you had not yet been introduced to myself," the lady replied, stumbling only a little over her first few words as she came up with a somewhat plausible explanation. "I am glad now that we have become acquainted, Lord Stratham."

Her eyes drifted over his face once more, lingering on his scar for long moments and without any attempt to hide such a thing from his view either. Frederick remained steadfast, refusing to be quelled by such a thing and thinking silently to himself that Lady Kingham was, quite certainly, one of the most shameless and, indeed, discourteous ladies that he had ever had the opportunity to meet. He could only hope that Lady Georgina had not hidden *her* true nature from him and that she did not take after her mother in this particular regard!

Clearing his throat, Frederick folded his arms and tilted his head just a little, waiting until Lady Kingham had met his gaze before he spoke again. Now was the time to be bold, to play his hand, and to make certain that his acquaintance with Lady Georgina – such as it was – could be used to his advantage.

"I should very much like to call on your daughter, Lady Kingham," he said, in as pleasant a voice as he could. "You would permit me to do so, I hope?"

He saw the flash of uncertainty in Lady Kingham's eyes but, given the circumstances, and the fact that Lady

Kellingston was still present, Lady Kingham had no choice but to consent.

"But of course, Lord Stratham." Her smile was tight, her teeth a little bared. "We would be *very* glad to have you call." Her eyes darted to Frederick's right and, after a moment, none other than Lady Georgina drew near. "Ah, Georgina." Lady Kingham gestured to Frederick. "It seems that Lord Stratham is eager to call on you."

Her eyes remained fixed to her daughter, as though she expected her now to gently refuse such an offer, but much to Frederick's delight, Lady Georgina smiled with a bright and obvious happiness that could not be mistaken for anything else.

"How lovely," she answered, looking directly into Frederick's eyes. "I would be very glad to see you again whenever you have the opportunity to call."

She glanced towards her mother and, upon doing so, Frederick saw her lips quirk. His stomach dropped to the floor. Did Lady Georgina know that her mother disapproved of his connection to her? And was she only showing such eagerness in the hope of frustrating her mother in some way?

Why should it matter to you what Lady Georgina's intentions are? asked a small, quiet voice within him. *You are doing so only to discover whether or not Lord Kingham is the man involved with the French. Lady Georgina means nothing.*

Such thoughts filled him with a fresh determination and Frederick cleared his throat, choosing now to take his leave so that he would not have to remain to make awkward conversation.

"I shall call tomorrow, Lady Georgina," he said, sweeping

into a grand bow. "Good evening, Lady Kingham. Lady Georgina – until our dance." He turned to Lady Kellingston. "And good evening to you, Lady Kellingston," he finished, before turning on his heel and removing himself from their close presence. As he made his way back through the crowd, he spotted none other than the Duke of Abernyte, who was still surrounded by various ladies of the *ton*. Frederick threw him a glance, a grim smile, and a nod and saw the Duke nod in return.

Thus far, at least, Frederick had enjoyed success. He could only hope that, very soon, he would find himself acquainted with Lord Kingham and, in time, would be able to discover whether or not the man was involved with their enemy. His heart lurched suddenly as he turned towards the door, choosing to spend the rest of the Ball, apart from his promised dances with Lady Georgina and Lady Matilda, in the card room.

A vision of Lady Georgina, weeping and broken-hearted, filled his mind. If Lord Kingham *was* the man they sought, then the *ton* would turn on Lady Kingham and, thereafter, Lady Georgina. The entire family would be excluded from society, spurned, and rejected utterly, which would mean that Lady Georgina would have no prospects whatsoever. She would face a life of spinsterhood, forced to live a quiet and dull life, likely in poverty, knowing that she would never again be permitted to enjoy the status she had once held in society – and all because of the choices of her father.

You are being quite ridiculous.

Frederick drew in a deep breath and closed his eyes momentarily, giving himself a shake.

You do not know for certain if Lord Kingham is the one you seek and even if he is, there are ways and means to lessen the damage to Lady Kingham and her daughter.

Why he was so very concerned about Lady Georgina, Frederick could not say. It was quite ridiculous given that they had only just become acquainted, and he was not a man inclined towards foolishness. And yet, Frederick could not help but throw one more glance over his shoulder, knowing full well who it was his eyes searched for. They did find her, for Lady Georgina stood only a short distance away. For a moment, their eyes met and he held her gaze – and then the next, someone walked between them and she was gone from his sight.

The card room was hardly welcoming, as many of the men flinched from the sight of his face too, but no one said anything, and he simply stood there, watching the men play, listening carefully to both conversation, and the faint drift of the music from the other room. At the appointed time, he went back to the ballroom, and sought out lady Matilda for their dance, and then Lady Georgina for the following one.

She took his hand as they moved into place in readiness for the country dance and heat surged through him. In that moment, he was glad that she had given him this dance – which would keep them apart much of the time, moving and turning about each other, and the other couples. He was not sure how well he would have coped with a dance which had required him to hold her...

They spoke of very little as they danced, for the movements were energetic, and not conducive to conversation, but again, he was struck by the fact that she did not stare at his scar, or avoid his face – she simply met his eyes and smiled. It was a smile he could get used to seeing. The dance ended, and he bowed, escorted her back to her mother, and stepped away, finding himself in need of cool air.

He sought the terrace, and simply stood, staring up at

the stars. Again, that vision came to him, of a weeping Lady Georgina, should her father prove to be a traitor. That vision made him almost wish that duty did not require him to investigate anyone who might be 'Lord K'. After some time, he shook himself out of that gloom and turned back to the ballroom. He would go home – the rest of the evening suddenly held no appeal for him. As he moved across the ballroom, he saw her again, dancing, unsmiling, with another gentleman, and he wondered at her thoughts.

He shook his head – her thoughts were none of his business. He moved on across the room, nodding at Abernyte as he passed him, irritated with himself and yet glad that he had seen her one more time. He was not about to permit himself to become preoccupied with one pretty young lady, especially when he was uncertain of her motivations, her intentions, and her character! He could not afford to become distracted – not even for a moment – and Lady Georgina could be a very beautiful distraction if he permitted her to be. Letting out a long breath, Frederick stood on the front steps of the house and breathed in the cool night air. He would *not* lose his head... and even more than that, Frederick was determined that he would not lose his heart.

CHAPTER FIVE

*G*eorgina walked into the drawing-room, only to see none other than her father standing next to her mother, in evident close conversation. His head was close to hers and he was gesturing with one hand, whilst Lady Kingham stood with her head a little bowed, although Georgina noticed the dark frown which pulled at her mother's face.

"Pray excuse me," she murmured hastily, making to step back out of the room, only for her father to beckon her back in.

"Come in, Georgina," he said, in a tone that told her that she could not even *think* of arguing with him. "There is something we must discuss." Georgina nodded and came back into the room at once, although she did not miss the flash of evident triumph on her mother's face. "Your mother tells me that Lord Jeffries is seeking a closer acquaintance with you, my dear," her father said, looking from Lady Kingham to Georgina and back again. "Are you aware of this?"

A knot formed in Georgina's stomach.

"No, I am not, father," she answered, seeing how her mother lifted her chin just a little, clearly feeling quite certain of her victory in this. "Lord Jeffries is –"

"A *most* suitable gentleman," Lady Kingham interrupted, quickly. "He danced with you last evening, did he not?"

Georgina blinked quickly, her stomach now tight and painful as she realized what her mother had been talking of. No doubt she had been encouraging Lord Kingham to consider Lord Jeffries, to think well of him and to, in his own way, to encourage – if not force Georgina – to consider him also.

"He did, yes," she said, slowly, her eyes narrowing slightly. "Although, Mama, I did inform you that I have no interest in Lord Jeffries." She looked back at her father, noting the surprise in his expression, and feeling her heart sink low. Evidently, her mother had expressed otherwise, no doubt stating that Georgina had been more than interested in Lord Jeffries' company.

"No?" Lord Kingham replied, glancing at Lady Kingham and then back to Georgina. "Is there a reason why?"

"Why does such a thing as Georgina's opinion matter?" Lady Kingham interrupted, brusquely. "Lord Jeffries is a *perfect* match for her, and given that she has already rejected Lord Newton–"

"Lord Jeffries is an arrogant oaf who thinks only of himself and gives not even a single thought to another living soul," Georgina stated, all too aware that she had broken into her mother's speaking but choosing to defend herself rather than do as propriety instructed by waiting until Lady

Kingham had finished speaking. "When we danced last evening, he spoke most unkindly about one or two of the other young ladies and–"

Lady Kingham swiped the air with her hand.

"That is only because he was attempting to impress you!" she cried, as though this somehow forgave Lord Jeffries for his harsh words. "He wanted to make quite certain that *you* were the one best thought of in his eyes, and this was his way of showing that to you!"

Georgina shook her head violently as her father remained silent, his eyes watchful. He never took any interest in Georgina and her considerations when it came to the various gentlemen who might consider her but, for whatever reason, her mother had now thought it best to involve him – most likely because she did not like Georgina continually rejecting those whom she thought to be excellent matches.

"Lord Jeffries is not the sort of gentleman I could *ever* consider tying myself to," she stated, outright. "Nor is Lord Newton. I do not understand why there is such an eagerness for me to choose one of the gentlemen whom you suggest, Mama! *I* am the one who must find a husband, am I not? And then live with them for the rest of my life? Therefore, should it not be my decision? Surely there should be a willingness to understand my dislike, rather than an irritation or upset?"

"Do be careful, Georgina." Lord Kingham took a small step closer, looking at Georgina with sharp eyes. "Your mother seeks only the best for you. She is correct to state that this is not your first Season and that, as time passes, you might be considered less and less by the gentlemen of the *ton*. After all, if you have not wed by your third Season–"

"This is only my second Season though, father," Georgina replied, making things all the worse for herself by interrupting Lord Kingham in her eagerness. "Surely there cannot be any great haste!"

Lord Kingham's brows knotted together.

"Your mother has come to me with a complaint about your conduct, Georgina," he stated, unequivocally. "And given the manner in which you have behaved these last few minutes, I can see why she is so eager for you to wed. A gentleman might think well of you at present, but if you are allowed to continue in this manner, then all of society will reject you! And no gentleman would wish to have a head-strong, opinionated young lady for a bride!"

His words stung, and Georgina took a step back as though she had been struck. Her face reddened and she felt tears prick the corners of her eyes, but an inner strength continued to grow. She knew full well that if she did nothing, if she did not speak up and plead her case, then she would be forced into a marriage with someone akin to Lord Newton or Lord Jeffries.

"I quite understand what you are saying, Father," she began, speaking quietly and with a good deal more care. "However, if I might be able to express my own opinion in this, I would be grateful."

A harsh sound came from her mother's lips.

"There is no need to attempt to justify yourself, Georgina," she answered, before Lord Kingham could say anything. "Your father knows all."

Georgina closed her eyes and drew in a long breath.

"Please, Father," she said, softly. "I know that there is more that needs to be said." Opening her eyes, she looked directly back at her father. "For example, has mother told you that there have been gentlemen I have suggested – gentlemen I have been eager to further my acquaintance with – but that I have been refused permission to even consider them?" She did not want to speak poorly about her mother but knew that she had to make her father aware of all that was going on. "Even last evening, there was a gentleman–"

"Georgina, stop!" Lady Kingham's eyes had flared wide, her hands held palms up and outward towards Georgina. "You cannot even *think* of–"

"Please, my dear." Lord Kingham frowned, putting one hand on Lady Kingham's arm, although his eyes remained fixed to Georgina's. "There was a gentleman last evening, you say?"

A wave of relief poured over Georgina.

"Yes, Father," she said, softly, glad that she had her chance to speak. "He is a suitable gentleman in terms of his status and title, for he is a Marquess."

"But he is *quite* unsuitable," her mother interrupted. "He bears an injury – a mark – Lord Kingham, and it is so very apparent that all of the *ton* talk of it!" She threw up her hands. "Could you imagine our daughter being connected with such a fellow?"

Lord Kingham said nothing in response to either Georgina or Lady Kingham. Instead, he simply kept his frown fixed in place as he looked from one lady to the other. Georgina chose to say nothing more, praying that what her mother had said would be enough to give Lord Kingham pause.

"An injury, you say?" Lord Kingham murmured, eventually. "Are you speaking of Lord Stratham, mayhap?" One brow lifted. "I have heard that he has returned from war."

Lady Kingham nodded furiously, clearly relieved that her husband knew what she spoke of.

"That is the very same gentleman," she stated, firmly. "Could you imagine it, my Lord?"

Lord Kingham's frown seemed to grow all the more as he looked from Lady Kingham to Georgina and back again.

"I think," he said, eventually, as Georgina's stomach cramped in the most discomfiting manner, "that to refuse to consider a gentleman who has been at war, who has fought for King and country and, in doing so, been injured severely, is a very grave mistake." Georgina could not take in his answer for a few moments, staring at her father with wide eyes as her mother did the very same, although clearly with more horror and upset in her expression than Georgina! "Lord Stratham is, from what I understand, a gentleman who is well respected, honorable, and coura-geous," Lord Kingham continued, his chin lifting. "If he is truly a gentleman whom you wish to consider, Georgina, then I have no objection. And neither does your mother."

"I..."

Lady Kingham's mouth had opened as though to refute this particular remark, only to close again, cutting off her words, as she took in her husband's severe expression. Her eyes closed tightly but she nodded as she did so, allowing Georgina to breathe a little more easily.

"I think, Georgina, that you are to be commended for such a consideration, in fact," Lord Kingham added, speaking a little more quietly now. "A gentleman whom the *ton* will consider to be less than favorable given his injury is not a gentleman that *you* ignore, it seems." A glimmer of a smile caught his lips and Georgina felt like weeping. It was the first time that her father had, in any way, commended her for something she had either done or said, and she did not quite know how to take it in. "Your mother and I have some more to discuss but, at present, you are not to be forced towards Lord Jeffries." His smile faded. "Although you must continue to watch your conduct, Georgina. I do not want your mother to be displeased with you."

"Yes, Father." Georgina's voice was hoarse with relief, her eyes looking nowhere but into her father's face for fear that, if she looked elsewhere, he would think her poorly behaved. She dared not glance at her mother, feeling a great trepidation about what she would see there, knowing that Lady Kingham was displeased, but not wanting to add anything further to such disapproval. "I – I will excuse myself now."

Lord Kingham nodded and then immediately turned to Lady Kingham, who closed her eyes once more, placed a hand over them, and waved her other one frantically as though to push her husband aside. Georgina hurried from the room, not wanting to remain or to see what took place next, quite certain that her father would not permit Lady Kingham to ignore him. There would be a long conversation between them, she was sure, but Georgina was glad to know now that it would not be about which gentleman they ought to foist upon their daughter. In this matter, at least, she had won a slight reprieve.

Do I really consider Lord Stratham to be a suitable match?

The thought played on her mind as Georgina made her way to the front of the house, sending for a maid so that she might take a short walk, in the park in the middle of the square, before afternoon calls began. Lord Stratham had come to her mind as she had stood before her mother and father and Georgina had not hesitated to mention him. They had only been introduced last evening and yet

Georgina had thought him to be everything a gentleman ought. He was respectable, well-mannered, danced well, and whilst his conversation had not flowed easily, he had made a good attempt at it. No doubt, Lord Stratham did not have very many young ladies to converse with, given his current situation, so she could forgive him for finding it a little difficult.

But do you truly think well of him?

Her lips twisted as she stepped out onto the London street. She had not made up her mind about Lord Stratham but, if he proved to be just as gentlemanly as she expected, then there was no reason she could not think of him as a suitable match... especially given that her father thought so well of him! It would be her mother who would object the most, but Georgina could deal with that without too much difficulty.

That is, if he would have me!

The thought made her smile and Georgina continued on her walk at a leisurely pace, thinking of all that her father had said, and finding herself quite filled with both delight and relief. To know that her father thought well of something she had done, something she had said, was a great joy indeed. Lord Kingham had said very little to her, or of her, in all the years of her life, and now, to hear him say something good had filled Georgina's heart in a way that she had never felt before. Her smile remained as she continued her walk, allowing herself the freedom to choose her steps as she wished, winding through the paths of the park.

"Good afternoon, Lady Georgina!"

Georgina stopped quickly, having been entirely unaware of who else was in the park with her, and only just then realizing that none other than Lord Stratham now stood before her.

"I – I was just on my way to call upon you," he said, stammering a little awkwardly as he looked from his right to his left as though in search of an explanation for why she was out of doors when afternoon calls were soon to take place. "I am a little early, I will admit, which is why I chose to walk in the park for a short while, but such was my eagerness that..." Closing his eyes tightly, he shook his head. "Forgive me," he continued. "That is to say, I did not wish to be early for any other reason than to make certain of my visit."

It was as though he did not want her to think that he was being overeager but this in itself satisfied Georgina immensely. He was a considerate gentleman, it seemed, and she thought well of him for it.

"I am just about to return home, Lord Stratham," she said, smiling at him as he looked back at her. "I came for a short walk before afternoon calls, for as you know, they can often be somewhat tedious depending on how many callers there are, or calls to make!"

She laughed, her eyes twinkling and Lord Stratham – after a moment – allowed his smile to spread wide across his face.

"I quite understand, Lady Georgina," he answered, touching his hat for a moment. "Might I be permitted to accompany you back to your townhouse?" He looked all about him again, before his eyes finally landed on the maid who was trailing in her wake. "Indeed, I would be very glad to do so."

Georgina nodded, turned, and was a little surprised when he offered her his arm. Clearly, he had considered the situation to be quite proper now that he had seen the maid who was present and had thus decided now to offer her his arm so that they might walk together. There came a small, warm pleasure in her heart as she accepted it, walking alongside him as they made their way back through the park and across the street.

"Might I ask you if you often think of London society as so very dull, Lady Georgina?"

Looking sharply at Lord Stratham for a moment, Georgina saw the gleam in his eye and realized that he was teasing her just a little.

"I have given myself away, have I not?" she asked, her lips lifting in a small smile. "In referring to both receiving and making afternoon calls as tedious, I have stated outright that I am a trifle bored by the rigmarole which comes with being part of the *ton*." She sighed a little discontentedly, surprised at how open she was able to be with him. "I have been here in London for two Seasons now and find that there is much required of young ladies." Her lips twisted but she continued to speak without hesitation, finding his company a gentle and inviting presence. "It is difficult to go about the same things, in the same manner, and with the same expectations, over and over again."

"Difficult and somewhat dull, I must imagine."

Georgina laughed, aware of how Lord Stratham was repeating her own words.

"Indeed, indeed," she replied, twinkling at him. "But it is not right for a young lady to say such things, so we must speak of something else, Lord Stratham, before I quite repulse you."

Lord Stratham chuckled, the sound rich as he smiled back at her.

"I hardly think that you could do such a thing, Lady Georgina," he responded. "In fact, I think it would be quite impossible."

A little taken aback at his response, Georgina did not know what to say, and some moments of awkwardness passed as they walked together. Clearing her throat, Georgina hurried to try to think of what she might speak of next.

"My father is aware of your return to London, Lord Stratham," she eventually said, thinking it best for Lord Stratham to know that her father thought well of him, since, from her mother's conduct last evening, it was clear that Lady Kingham did not. "He states that you were at war?"

Lord Stratham's head spun sharply towards her.

"I beg your pardon?"

His tone took her by surprise, for there was a sharpness there that could not be mistaken. Her breath caught in her chest for a moment as she looked up into his face, seeing the steadiness in his eyes and the tightness about his lips.

Clearly, he does not wish to be reminded of the war, she thought to herself, shrugging one shoulder as she spoke in response.

"I do not mean to speak out of turn, Lord Stratham," she said, softly, "it is only that my father mentioned that you were at war and had returned to London. That is all."

Lord Stratham did not immediately respond. His head turned away from hers, his brows began to knot together, and he nodded slowly, perhaps thinking carefully about what she had said. Georgina remained silent, cursing herself for speaking without true consideration. Of course Lord Stratham would not want to be reminded of the war! After all, the scar to his face was the very reason that the *ton* wanted to remain far from him, why they considered him to be less than worthy. It had been foolish of her to mention it. A little embarrassed by her blunder, Georgina remained quite silent, her head dipping a little lower.

"Forgive me, Lady Georgina." Lord Statham's voice was

filled with apology. "I spoke a little harshly there. I did not mean to do so."

"You need not apologize, Lord Statham," Georgina replied, quickly. "I ought to apologize for being thoughtless in my remarks. Of course, you will not want to discuss the war." She glanced up at him and then looked away again. "It must have been terrible."

Another sharp look up towards him showed a gentleman with a somewhat twisted expression, his eyes appearing thoughtful, but his lips bunched together as though he were not quite certain what to say next, even though Georgina was quite certain that his mind must be filled with all manner of thoughts. She continued to walk silently, thinking it best to wait until Lord Statham himself spoke. Her consideration of Lord Statham's character, however, grew steadily for, whilst he had been perturbed by what she had said, he had gone on to apologize for his remarks, as though *he* were the one in the wrong! Georgina's lips curved into a soft smile. Lord Statham had greater merits than she had first thought.

"The war held a great many horrors, yes," Lord Statham began eventually, his voice filled with an emotion which he did not express in words. "The truth is, Lady Georgina, I did not want to leave it. Despite the pain, despite the suffering that I have witnessed, despite the torment that I knew so many faced, there was still a desire in me to remain." His head turned towards her, and his eyes beseeched her to understand in some small part, even though Georgina knew that she could not know fully what he expressed. "I wanted to stay so that I might continue to fight for my King and my country," he finished, heavily. "Not to return here, where so many look at me and think less of me because of the small injury I bear."

Georgina's heart lurched with sympathy for him.

"*I* do not think less of you, Lord Statham," she said, softly. "The injury you speak of with such careless terms must, I think, have been very painful at the time."

A harsh, guttural sound came from Lord Statham's lips.

"It is only a trifle compared to what others experienced," he said, heavily. "Lady Georgina, I would not describe the despair and the pain that I have witnessed for fear of upsetting you, but needless to say, many men have lost far more than their handsome looks." He shook his head, his lips tight. "My injury is nothing compared to them."

Regarding him carefully, Georgina lifted one shoulder.

"You have done a great deal, I am sure," she said, quietly. "They would not have insisted you return to London without good reason."

Again, a sound came from Lord Statham which Georgina did not quite understand. It was somewhere between a laugh and a cry, his lips pulling in a sorrowful smile.

"They insisted that I return, because I am a gentleman, a nobleman of the realm without an heir at present and that, as such, I must be protected," he said, his voice and eyes hard. "Any other man who had suffered as I did would have been patched up and then returned to their position, so that they might continue to fight for King and country." He shrugged, spreading out his free hand in front of him. "*I*, however, was returned almost at once, given my status and position. It would not do for a Marquess to be killed."

A little surprised at the bitterness in his tone, Georgina chose to consider his words silently for some time rather than immediately respond. Lord Stratham threw her a glance, but she merely gave him a quick smile, letting her mind run through all that he had said and allowing herself to consider it carefully. Lord Stratham, it seemed, was a gentleman of honor. He did not want to be removed from his position simply because of his title. In fact, he appeared upset that he had been forced into such action, clearly preferring to have remained exactly where he was so that he might serve the King. How many other gentlemen could say that? Georgina knew that many used their position and their title in any way they could so that they might best others and take full advantage of all that could be offered to them. Lord Stratham, it seemed, was not such a gentleman and that lifted him even higher in her estimation.

"There must be some things you can do still, Lord Stratham," she said, as they approached the house. "The war effort will still need great minds to come up with secure strategies for battle and the like?" She smiled at him and laughed as he lifted one eyebrow, her cheeks coloring just a little. "I speak none of what I know, of course, for I do not understand all that is required of those in war. But I must pray that there is something here that you can do, Lord Stratham. It must pain you greatly to be so far from battle."

He looked back at her, his eyes holding something that she could not quite make out.

"It does, Lady Georgina," he replied, quietly. "But you are quite correct, there are some things that I can help with whilst remaining here in London. It is not quite the same as being close to the enemy, but it is better than having to return to society without even a whisper of what is going on!"

Georgina laughed softly.

"Is society so very bad, Lord Stratham?" Seeing his arched eyebrow, she shook her head and gave him a wry smile. "I suppose that it is, given how you have been treated. I am sorry for that, Lord Stratham."

"Pray, do not be," he answered, letting go of her arm as they came to the front door. "Your company and conversation, Lady Georgina, have pushed aside all my upset and irritation at being in amongst the rudest and most ill-mannered of society." His smile lifted so that it reached his eyes. "A smile from you has brightened my time here in London, to the point that I now find myself looking forward to entering society in case you are present."

A faint blush caught Georgina's cheeks and she did not answer, save for a warm smile, before she entered the house. To be so affected by Lord Stratham's remarks was quite unexpected and it took Georgina a few moments to compose herself. This short walk with him had revealed not only far more about the gentleman but also a good deal about her own inclination towards him. When she had spoken to her father earlier that afternoon, Georgina had mentioned Lord Stratham merely as an example, having been pressed into doing so – but now, she realized that there might be much more to their acquaintance than she had ever anticipated. Indeed, if their connection continued, if he appeared all the more agreeable, and she found herself continuing to consider him in this very same manner, then Georgina had to admit that she might not be averse to accepting Lord Stratham's court, should he ask her.

A small smile quirked her mouth as she walked into the drawing-room, ready to announce Lord Stratham's arrival to her mother. Should Lady Kingham be able to read her thoughts and see into her heart, then Georgina could not even imagine what her mother might say to her current state of mind!

"Lord Stratham, Mama," she said, turning back towards the gentleman. "We met just as I returned home."

She smiled back at him and then went to ring the bell, leaving her mother to welcome Lord Stratham just as graciously as she could. Her heart was more settled than when she had left the house for her walk and that, Georgina realized, was mostly due to the company of Lord Stratham.

CHAPTER SIX

"There is also Lord Coleshill."

Frederick threw a frown towards the Duke, who was sitting in his study chair, his feet stretched out and propped up on the desk in front of him.

"Lord Coleshill does not begin with the required letter."

The Duke of Abernyte chuckled, his eyes dancing.

"I was making certain that you were paying attention to me, Stratham," he replied, one eyebrow lifting in an questioning glance. "You have been a little preoccupied."

Frederick did not reply, but instead merely shrugged and then turned back towards the window. He looked out onto the street below and deliberately brought to mind how he had walked with Lady Georgina yesterday afternoon. Their walk had not been of a particularly long duration, but he had enjoyed it immensely, even though he was a little irritated, still, at how he had reacted when she had spoken of the war.

"Stratham?"

Clearing his throat, Frederick turned back to the Duke, spreading his hands.

"Yes?"

"What do you think?"

A faint heat began to rise in Frederick's chest, spreading up his neck and into his face as he realized that the Duke had said something that he was entirely unaware of, given that his thoughts had been entirely taken up with Lady Georgina.

"I –," he began, trying desperately to bring some answer to mind that would not betray what he had really been thinking of. "Yes, I think so. I would agree."

"You agree that Lord Coleshill is a gentleman we ought to consider?"

Frederick frowned, his lighthearted manner fading.

"What? No, no, I do not think we ought to consider him."

"Then why did you agree?"

Sighing heavily, Frederick turned from the window entirely, a wry smile pulling at his lips.

"Yes, very well, I am preoccupied with another matter," he stated, seeing the Duke's triumphant grin. "I was walking with Lady Georgina yesterday afternoon and –"

"Indeed!" The Duke sat bolt upright in an instant, swinging his legs down to the floor. "I have heard that she is a very outspoken creature but that might not be of any difficulty to you."

"It is not," Frederick replied, hastily. "But that is not what I mean. She mentioned her father and that *he* had spoken of my part in the war effort." He waited for the Duke to take this in, seeing the excited eagerness that had been in his friend's expression immediately begin to fade. "Evidently, Lord Kingham thinks quite highly of me... that is, at least according to Lady Georgina."

A frown knotted the Duke's brows.

"You have never met this gentleman, then?"

"I am not acquainted with him, no." Frederick shrugged. "It may be that he *is* aware of me and the reason for this." He gestured to his face. "Or it may be that he is aware of my part in the war for a different reason entirely."

Nodding slowly, the Duke rose to his feet and began to walk up and down the room.

"I have spoken to the three other gentlemen I know who have titles beginning with that letter – and whilst my investigations are ongoing, I would be surprised if any of them proved to be involved in some way." His lip curled. "Lord Kent, for example, is much too inclined to the drink, whilst Lord Knightsbridge is too aged." He looked back at Frederick sharply. "You *are* to call on Lady Georgina again, are you not? You must seek an introduction to her father."

Frederick nodded.

"I am," he replied, with a slight lift of his brows. "In fact, I have been invited to dine with them tomorrow evening!"

He chuckled as the Duke of Abernyte stared back at him for a moment, only to then grin widely.

"Even better!" he exclaimed, as a knock on the door interrupted them. "You will *certainly* be introduced to Lord Kingham there!"

Frederick waited until the Duke had answered the door, only to rise to his feet as another gentleman stepped in. Frederick had not been acquainted with him before but evidently, the Duke was not only acquainted with him but had been expecting him, given the way that the butler had simply ushered the fellow in without introduction.

"Ah, Lord Brinsworth!"

Frederick's ears pricked up at once, recalling how the Duke had told him that there would be another military gentleman returning from the war, whom they might be able to make use of. Lord Brinsworth bowed as the Duke introduced him to Frederick, as Frederick did the very same. Lifting his head, he took in the red-haired man and was not at all surprised to see a haunted expression in his grey eyes. Frederick knew all too well what could trouble one's soul during times of war.

"Sit, Lord Brinsworth, please."

As the man nodded and made his way to a chair, Frederick noted with a small flicker of surprise just how badly the fellow limped. He wanted to get up and offer to fetch Lord Brinsworth a cane or some such thing but made certain to refrain, knowing that to do so could cause great insult. Lord Brinsworth was determined to get about without such a thing and yet, at the same time, was struggling with a good deal of pain – it was etched about his eyes and in the tightness of his lips.

"You have both been sent back to London due to injury," the Duke stated as Lord Brinsworth eased himself into a chair. "Lord Stratham here is not at all contented with being back in London, just as I believe you are not either."

Lord Brinsworth flashed a quick, assessing look towards Frederick, as though he were not quite certain whether or not he could be trusted, before shrugging and looking away.

"Regardless of how I feel about being sent back to London, I would be very glad indeed if you could inform me of how I might be of use here," he stated, his tone low and steady. "I am not inclined towards dancing and the like."

Frederick chuckled and the atmosphere in the room lightened considerably.

"I quite understand," he replied, "but there may be a need for you to take part in such things."

The Duke nodded.

"Indeed," he began, before going into a quick explanation of all that had taken place and the new information they had been given. "Therefore, I am using my connections to make certain that I am acquainted with as many gentlemen as possible, whose title begins with a 'K,'" he finished. "Lord Stratham is doing the same, although his connection is with Lord Kingham's daughter at present, and not yet Lord Kingham."

"That will soon change," Frederick added, quickly. "But there are still a few others within the *ton* who will need to be considered. After all, this is of such importance that we cannot forget a single one. We *must* find who this 'Lord K' is, if we are to protect England."

"Given that this particular fellow has been instrumental in other attacks – including the attempt to poison me – we must find him," the Duke added. "Might you aid us, Lord Brinsworth?"

It took only a moment for Lord Brinsworth to nod.

"But of course." His tone had lightened just a fraction and, whilst he did not smile, there was not a tightness about his lips any longer. "Whatever is required of me, I would be happy to do."

"Capital, I –"

A tap at the door interrupted them and, although the Duke frowned in displeasure, he called for the butler to enter. However, the butler was not the one who stepped inside when the door opened, but rather a small, somewhat disheveled fellow whom Frederick recognized at once. It was one of the men in his employ – James, if he recalled correctly. Being small in stature and very wiry, the man found it easy to make his way about without being seen – a skill which Frederick found invaluable.

"Lord Stratham." James ducked his head. "Forgive me, but I have something of importance to say."

Frederick spread out one hand.

"Please." He gestured to the Duke and Lord Brinsworth. "These men can be trusted so you may speak freely."

James nodded, his eyes darting from left to right.

"I do not know this gentleman's name," he said, apologetically, "but I must tell you that he has been followed to this house."

Blinking rapidly, Frederick looked at Lord Brinsworth, who had gone suddenly very still, staring at James fixedly.

"You mean to say that Lord Brinsworth is the one who has been followed?" he asked, as the man nodded. "You are quite certain."

"Entirely," the man replied, firmly. "The same fellow is waiting now for Lord Brinsworth to take his leave."

Frederick nodded, thanking James, and then dismissing him, one brow lifting as he looked from the Duke to Lord Brinsworth and back again.

"It seems that our enemy is aware of your presence here in London," the Duke murmured, as Lord Brinsworth frowned hard. "They have come to see if there is a connection between us and, knowing now that you are here and that Lord Stratham is present also, I must believe now that there are those in the *ton* who must know that we are still working for the war effort."

"*Your* part in things has been well known in society," Frederick pointed out. "I had hoped that our connection would not be so keenly observed, but it seems that with the return of Lord Brinsworth, suspicions have been raised."

Lord Brinsworth nodded firmly.

"Then we must know our enemy," he said, gruffly.

"That means that we are to find this 'Lord K' with all haste, given that we have nothing else to achieve at present. No other names, no other places that we must explore." He sighed and passed one hand over his eyes. "We are at a disadvantage, given that we will now be closely observed, no doubt."

"If not worse," Frederick murmured, his brows knotting as he thought of just how ruthless their enemy could be. "We must all be on our guard." He looked first to the Duke and then to Lord Brinsworth, seeing them both nod. "It is imperative to our safety."

"Agreed," the Duke replied, his voice low. "The battle is not yet over."

$$\approx$$

"Good evening, Lady Georgina."

Frederick could not help but be dazzled by the lady, despite firmly telling himself that the only reason he was here this evening was to be introduced to Lord Kingham.

"Good evening, Lord Stratham," Lady Georgina replied, her eyes sparkling like the diamonds she wore about her neck. "I am so very glad that you could join us this evening."

"But of course," he answered, smiling back at her. "It was a very kind invitation."

Lady Georgina's lips pulled into a wry smile.

"And a somewhat unexpected one, I must think." Seeing his look of surprise, she laughed. "My dear Lord Stratham, you need not think that I am entirely unaware of my mother's poor conversation, lack of eagerness to have your company here or, at times, her rude manner." Her smile faded and, much to Frederick's surprise, she reached out and pressed his arm for a moment. "I am sorry for it."

It took him a few moments to respond, his arm warm where her fingers had pressed.

"I – I do not think that *you* need to apologize, Lady Georgina," he said, a little clumsily. "Not that I expect your mother to apologize, of course." Closing his eyes tightly, he let out a wry exclamation. "Goodness, I am not speaking well this evening!"

Her laugh made his embarrassment fade.

"You are doing very well, Lord Stratham," she responded, as he looked back at her. "I should be glad to introduce you to my father at some point this evening also, given that he thinks well of you, and, after all, it would be nice if *one* of my parents did so!"

This was accompanied by a tiny wink and Frederick instantly felt heat pour into every single part of his being at such a coy gesture. He tried to laugh but the sound was brittle and dry, leaving Lady Georgina in a somewhat awkward state. There was no immediate response from either of them, with both of them feeling a trifle embarrassed, which Frederick tried to end by clearing his throat abruptly and then gesturing to a footman to bring him a glass of whatever it was that he held on his tray.

"Champagne," Lady Georgina said helpfully, as she too took a glass. "Not ratafia, in case that was what you feared!"

"Ratafia has never been my favorite concoction, I will admit," Frederick replied, the awkwardness between them gone. "But it is tolerable enough. Champagne, however..." He raised his glass and took a small sip, before nodding and smiling back at Lady Georgina. "That is excellent."

"I am glad you think so."

A voice from over his shoulder made Frederick start but he turned swiftly, gathering his composure as best he could.

"Oh, Father," Lady Georgina said quickly, coming to stand to the side of her father as the other guests continued to mingle around them. "Might I introduce the Marquess of Stratham?" She turned to Frederick. "Lord Stratham, my father, the Earl of Kingham."

Frederick kept his eagerness from his expression.

"Lord Kingham," he said, bowing low. "Good evening. I am very glad to make your acquaintance at last."

It had been somewhat peculiar to be invited to a dinner party without having ever been introduced to the host, but Frederick had accepted it without question. After all, he had been introduced to both Lady Georgina and Lady Kingham already! Lord Kingham was a tall, slightly imposing figure, who had thinning grey hair, a large, well-shaped moustache, and icy blue eyes. Frederick did not think that even a smile would give any warmth to such an expression.

"As I am to make yours," Lord Kingham replied, rising from his bow. "My daughter and my wife have both spoken of you and I am very glad to have finally become acquainted. Forgive me for not pursuing such a thing earlier, I have been rather busy with all manner of things." He waved a hand, a small smile pulling at his otherwise serious appearance. "You know how things can be."

"I do, indeed," Frederick replied, in what he hoped was a rueful manner. "A gentleman is always taken up with some matter or another."

"Precisely," Lord Kingham replied, his eyes still fixed on Frederick's expression.

Taking in a small yet deep breath, Frederick chose to be

bold and speak plainly. After all, given what had happened that afternoon, he had no time to be hesitant.

"I understand from your daughter that you are aware of my time fighting for the King," he said, as Lord Kingham's expression remained exactly as it had always been. "I am grateful for your understanding."

He lifted one hand to the side of his face, indicating his long scar, and saw the Earl nod.

"But of course," he replied, as Lady Georgina stood quietly, listening without hesitation. "Yes, I had heard of your return to London and the reason for it. I am sorry that you were pushed from the front lines without any opportunity to do otherwise. That must have been very trying for you."

Frederick nodded.

"It was," he answered, wondering still where Lord Kingham had heard such a thing. "But I am here now, and doing all that I can to enjoy the Season regardless!"

Without having had any intention of doing so, his eyes drew to the left to where Lady Georgina stood, and Frederick found himself looking into her eyes, finding a flush burning in his cheeks as he realized what he was doing.

"That is good, Lord Stratham," Lord Kingham replied, although Frederick did note how his gaze lingered on his daughter for a few moments. "I do hope that you will continue to enjoy society and that there will be less and less of those who seek to turn their back on you for nothing other than their own foolish judgments."

"I am grateful for the understanding that I *do* receive," Frederick said, as warmly as he could, although his sentiment did nothing to Lord Kingham's expression. "Thank you, Lord Kingham."

The man nodded, excused himself, and took his leave,

preparing to speak to his other guests. Frederick let out a long, slow breath, which he hid from Lady Georgina as best he could, all too aware of the tension now running through him. Would Lord Kingham speak so openly about his awareness of Frederick's past difficulties concerning the war and returning to London if he were doing all he could to keep his connection to the French a secret? Frederick could not believe so, although he was not about to rule out the idea entirely. After all, the gentleman could be foolhardy or think himself to be more secure than he truly was. Or, mayhap, he was attempting to let Frederick know that he had far more awareness and knowledge than even Frederick himself had expected.

"I – I should speak to some other guests."

Frederick's attention was caught by Lady Georgina, and he realized, much to his chagrin, that he had been standing quietly and had said nothing for some moments – no doubt leaving Lady Georgina with a rather dull and staid companion!

"Forgive me, Lady Georgina, I –"

"It is my duty only, Lord Stratham." Again, her hand came to rest on his arm, her eyes looking into his with such an appeal that Frederick caught his breath, hardly able to breathe for a few moments. "Thank you for your conversation and for being so gracious to my father."

"Thank you for introducing him, Lady Georgina," Frederick replied, still feeling a little foolish at how quickly he had been drawn into his own thoughts. "But you are quite correct, I have monopolized more of your time than I ought." He smiled and spread out one hand. "The other guests will be quite angry with me should you stay longer."

She laughed, her hand falling from his arm.

"I wanted to make certain that you were comfortable

here, Lord Stratham," she replied before he could say anything more. "And, in addition, I wanted the *ton* to see that you are just as welcomed and just as accepted as they are." Taking a small step closer, she leaned forward. "Do not let anyone speak down to you here, Lord Stratham," she finished softly. "Not even my mother."

Frederick could not quite summon a reply, but seeing her smile and the warmth in her eyes, satisfied himself with simply catching her hand and bowing over it before she took her leave. It was a small gesture, but not one that was lost on Lady Georgina. Her cheeks colored but her smile lingered, making Frederick sigh contently within. Watching her take her leave of him so that she might go and speak with others, Frederick drew in a deep breath and willed his heart to stop slamming so hard into his chest. After all, he told himself fiercely, Lady Georgina was nothing more than a means to an end. He ought not to be allowing himself to feel such things, to speak such things, and to be more desperate for her company than any other.

And yet, Frederick noted, shaking his head to himself, *I find myself jealous that she is gone to speak to the other guests present this evening.*

It was a foolish emotion indeed and Frederick tried to remove it from his mind but found that it was determined to stick to his very soul. Turning his head away from Lady Georgina, he looked around him and went towards another gentleman that he recognized. This evening's task had been completed, for he was now acquainted with Lord Kingham and therefore, he need do nothing more than enjoy the evening as best he could.

Especially if it means being in Lady Georgina's presence, said a quiet voice in his heart which, as much as Frederick tried to ignore it, grew steadily louder. *You are intrigued by her, are you not? Interested, eager, and much too caught up with her.*

That, Frederick had to admit, was quite true. He had to forget the lady, had to push all thought of her aside, and focus entirely on discovering the political leanings of Lord Kingham. Would he be for the King or the French? And if it was the latter, just how was Frederick going to explain it to Lady Georgina?

CHAPTER SEVEN

*G*eorgina sighed to herself contentedly as she stepped out of the front door and made her way to the carriage. It was a very pleasant afternoon and, whilst she was a little fatigued from last evening, that would not hold her back from taking an enjoyable ride in the carriage.

Stepping inside, Georgina settled herself, leaned back against the squabs, and closed her eyes. There had been one particular enjoyment last evening and that had been her ongoing acquaintance with Lord Stratham. How very strange it was to find herself so interested in such a gentleman! She did not even notice the scar on his face anymore, for his character was so interesting to her that she found herself drawn to him in a way that she could not explain. For whatever reason, Georgina had become more eager to be in his company than with any other and had been glad to talk with him. She had tried to tell herself that it was simply because she did not want the rest of the guests to look down upon him and think little of his company, but in her heart, Georgina knew that it was not so. She spoke to Lord

Stratham entirely for herself, wanting to do so to deepen their connection and to find out more about him. He interested her and she had been able to speak without reserve, although whether or not such a thing had been wise, Georgina was not quite certain! To have spoken so of her mother had perhaps not been the best thing to say, but Georgina did not want to pretend that all was well as regarded her mother's attitude towards Lord Stratham. It was quite plain for him to see and to pretend that it was not there at all seemed foolish.

"Drive on."

Georgina spoke loudly as she rapped on the roof of the carriage, ready for the driver to make his way through London. Georgina was eager just to sit quietly and look out of her window at all that was going on, contented to be with her own thoughts. It was not often that she was alone – albeit, in the company of her maid – but she was grateful to be away from her mother for a time, who would otherwise have demanded to know who Georgina had spoken to last evening and, no doubt, what she thought of one or two particular gentlemen.

Lord Stratham would not have been in her considerations, Georgina thought to herself, a little sadly. *He is still not someone that my mother wishes me to consider.*

Georgina thought it quite ridiculous that someone could be so judged based solely on their appearance but that was, unfortunately, the way of the *ton*. How many young ladies had been noted for their lack of lace, an unnoticed tear in one of their gowns, or, worst of all, wearing the same gown twice! Grimacing, she continued to look out of the window, trying to push such unsettling thoughts from her mind so that she might instead think on more pleasant things.

Things such as Lord Stratham?

Her heart pressed hard into her chest for a moment as a delicious curl of excitement filled her, as though she expected to see him at any moment. It was a foolish emotion given that Georgina had no expectation of seeing the gentleman, only for her to suddenly realize that they were drawing close to his townhouse, the location of which she had heard mentioned by the gossips at one of the balls. Her eyes closed and she turned her head away, not wanting him to see her as the carriage made its way past the house. No doubt Lord Stratham would be busy elsewhere, perhaps making afternoon calls and therefore would not be at home to see her, but Georgina still felt the urge to turn away for fear that he would take note of her presence and wonder why she had been driven past his townhouse. It was another strange, awkward reaction and Georgina gave herself a small shake, telling herself that she needed to get hold of herself and her own foolish heart.

"You there!"

A loud shout startled her and, just as she was about to look out of the opposite window to see what was occurring, the door to her carriage flew open and a man she did not recognize jumped inside.

Georgina let out a cry of fright, only for the man to reach out and grab her sleeve.

"Out!" Georgina did not know how to react, staring at the man with unbridled horror. He had dark, unkempt hair which stuck up in all directions, a long narrow nose, sharp, almost-black eyes and lips which were pulled into an ugly sneer. "Out!"

His hand pulled at her again and Georgina was forced from her seat. The next moment, the carriage door was pulled open and, before she could react, Georgina found herself falling out. She landed on something – or someone, tumbling to the ground and finding dust – and likely worse - filling her nostrils and her mouth as she gasped for breath, the air around her seeming clammy. The sound of a gunshot rang through the air and Georgina let out a cry of horror, dropping her head back to the ground and covering herself with her hands, for fear that she would be attacked.

The sounds came thick and fast as Georgina kept her eyes shut tight, her whole body trembling with the shock of what had occurred. The scream of horses, the shouts of the men all about her, the cries of the women, and, as she listened, one voice coming through it all – one voice that she recognized.

Lord Stratham.

"Stay there, Lady Georgina," he was saying, only for Georgina to realize that his hand was now pressed to her back. "Stay for just a moment longer, until we are certain that..." He trailed off and Georgina dared a glance upwards, seeing him looking past her. She tried to sit up and Lord Stratham seemed to regain himself a little, looking down at her and immediately helping her up. There was a great crowd all about them and Georgina felt herself flush with embarrassment, only to let out a sharp cry of pain as she realized that her ankle ached terribly. She was covered with dust from head to foot and, on top of all this, had scrapes and bruises everywhere. "Might you permit me to help you into the house?"

Lord Stratham was already holding onto her arm tightly, but Georgina knew that he would have to do more than that were she to be helped inside. Looking around her and seeing the wide eyes and whispered words that were already coming from the onlookers, Georgina closed her eyes and prayed that she would not lose her good reputation to scandal.

"Pray, allow us *both* to assist."

Georgina looked up in surprise to see another gentleman drawing near, a gentleman she did not recognize.

"Lord Brinsworth, thank you," Lord Stratham murmured. "Lady Georgina, this is the Earl of Brinsworth who is the very best of gentlemen. If we can assist you together then I do not think you will have to be carried." A tiny smile lifted one corner of his mouth. "That is what was troubling you, no?"

Georgina nodded tightly and, much to her relief, both gentlemen were able to assist her into the house without either of them insisting on lifting her. She was able to put weight on her ankle, but it was with a heavy limp. Having the support of both Lord Stratham and Lord Brinsworth meant that she could tolerate it well enough.

"What happened?" she stammered, as she was placed gently down into one of the drawing-room armchairs, sinking back into its softness with relief. "My maid, she is still –"

"You may not have seen, Lady Georgina, but your maid exited the carriage before you did," Lord Stratham interrupted gently, clearly meaning to calm her anxiety. "She came shouting for help and, to be truthful, I almost knocked into her!" He smiled reassuringly. "My housekeeper already has her below stairs, making certain that she is recovering."

A wave of relief crashed over Georgina.

"What of the carriage?" she asked, just as two maids hurried into the room. "My coachman... I..."

Lord Stratham held out one hand to her, silently asking her to stem her questions for the moment.

"We must take care of you first, Lady Georgina," he said, with a little more firmness to his tone. "The Duke of Abernyte has gone in search of your carriage. It is very fortunate that he had only just arrived and, upon seeing what was happening, was able to return to his carriage and go in pursuit." He beckoned to one of his maids. "Now, I shall leave you in the care of my maids and the housekeeper, who will be with you in a moment. I must inform your father at once of what has occurred."

Before Lord Stratham could leave, Georgina reached out and grasped his hand, keeping him where he crouched next to her. His eyes looked into hers and Georgina was a little taken aback by the sheer amount of concern she read in his expression. Despite her pain, despite her shock, Georgina found herself greatly relieved that she had been in Lord Stratham's company.

"Lord Stratham," she began, her voice a little wispy, such was her surprise at seeing his alarm over her circumstances. "I thank you for your assistance. It must have been fate that had me directly outside your door when that... that... *ruffian*... entered my carriage. I cannot understand why...." Slowly, she trailed off, looking into Lord Stratham's face as a realization began to form in her mind. "Unless he...."

Lord Stratham patted her hand briskly with his other, clearing his throat as he did so.

"You *must* be attended to, Lady Georgina. I cannot permit it to be held back for even a moment longer."

Georgina made to say something more, but there was no time. Lord Stratham had moved away, giving her a short bow as he stood by Lord Brinsworth. The two maids and the housekeeper – who had suddenly appeared without Georgina seeing her – began to move in towards Georgina to assess her injuries.

"We will return shortly, Lady Georgina," Lord Stratham said, as the housekeeper tutted loudly over

Georgina's scraped hands. "Pray inform me when Lady Georgina is ready for us to speak to her again, Mrs. Gillingham."

This last sentence was spoken directly to the house-keeper, who nodded and then turned back to Georgina. Georgina was left helplessly watching as Lord Stratham and Lord Brinsworth departed, her mind now filled with questions which she did not think would soon be answered. A great weariness came over her as the maids began to clean her scraped hands and Georgina felt herself sink back even further into the chair. It had been a terrible afternoon and yet, despite the shock and the pain, Georgina was quite certain that there was more to what had occurred than simply a mere ruffian who had decided to steal her carriage. Georgina determined, then and there, that Lord Stratham himself would *have* to explain everything to her – whether he wished to or not.

~

"LADY GEORGINA, HOW ARE YOU?"

Georgina rose from her chair without difficulty, straight-ening her shoulders and ignoring the pain which stabbed her ankle as she did so.

"I am recovering well, Lord Stratham," she answered, her voice filled with determination and resolve. "Thank you for calling."

Lord Stratham bowed and then turned to Georgina's mother.

"Lady Kingham, I do hope that you also have recovered from the shock? I cannot imagine how terrible it must have been for you to see your daughter in such a state."

Casting her gaze towards Lady Kingham, Georgina was

surprised when a glisten of tears came into her mother's eyes. Lady Kingham had been steady and seemingly quite calm throughout, although she had been a little pale when Georgina had arrived home – brought in Lord Stratham's carriage and accompanied by her maid, who had also been quite shaken. Her father had been the one who had appeared horrified at what had occurred, showing more emotion and concern for Georgina than she had ever experienced from him before. Now, it seemed, Georgina's mother had kept much of what she had felt entirely to herself.

"I am well recovered, I thank you," Lady Kingham responded, in a tone which seemed to express genuine gladness at Lord Stratham's concern. "Thank you again, Lord Stratham, for all that you did in recovering my daughter and returning her home safely."

Georgina blinked in surprise but cast a warm smile in her mother's direction, glad that she was showing true gratitude and seemingly now thought rather more highly of Lord Stratham than before.

"It was not a great deal, I assure you," Lord Stratham said, waving a hand. "I am only glad that Lady Georgina has recovered so quickly."

He sent another smile in Georgina's direction and she returned it at once although her mind remained quite ready to put her plan into action. The moment she had known that Lord Stratham was to come to call, Georgina had given much thought to how she might bring about a particular situation. She wanted to be alone with Lord Stratham – or as alone as she could be – so that she might speak to him about what had occurred. The more she had thought of it, the more her shock had worn away, the more she had begun to realize that there might be far more to what had happened than she had first thought.

"I had thought about taking a drive in the carriage, mama," she said innocently, casting a quick smile towards Lady Kingham. "I know that Lord Stratham would not mind accompanying us, as it is a very fine afternoon." She was speaking very boldly indeed and making many assumptions, but one look at Lord Stratham told her that she had succeeded in her intentions, for he was nodding quickly. "I am very grateful to you for calling upon us, Lord Stratham, but I confess that I have spent many an hour sitting here in this chair these last few days, and to venture out would be pleasant!"

His eyes twinkled.

"All that sitting here must have been a little dull, I must have thought."

Georgina hid a smile, turning back towards her mother.

Lady Kingham frowned.

"It is near the fashionable hour, Georgina," she said, sounding a little reproachful. "You know that all of the *ton* are talking of you and what occurred. Do you truly wish to return to them in such a state as this?"

Georgina laughed, throwing aside her mother's concerns without hesitation.

"I am not unwell, Mama!" she exclaimed, reaching across to press her mother's hand lightly. "It would be good to show society that I am quite recovered, and not afraid, would it not?" She kept her smile in place and tilted her head to one side for a few moments. "I could, I suppose, stay in the carriage rather than walk out amongst everyone, if that would satisfy you?"

Again, Lady Kingham hesitated, but it was Lord Stratham who spoke first.

"I would be glad to take you both in my carriage," he

said, gallantly. "If that would please you, Lady Kingham, of course."

It took a few moments but, eventually, Lady Kingham consented. Georgina was very much relieved, although she had suspected that her mother would agree for, despite Lady Kingham's eagerness to make certain that Georgina was quite well and recovering, it had been a trial for them both to remain in the house instead of attending various society events. Lady Kingham was as much a social butterfly as she had ever been and, whilst she had attended to Georgina with great care, there had still been a few remarks made and sighs given about what events they had been missing. To be able now to walk amongst the *ton*, to have them speak to her about what had happened to Georgina and, in some ways, to be of a little more importance than before, given the whispers and gossip about Georgina's plight, was certain to hold a little interest for Lady Kingham!

"Well, that would be very pleasant, if Georgina is eager to do so," Lady Kingham replied, although there was still a hint of reluctance in her voice. "Thank you, Lord Stratham."

He made his way to the door.

"I will have the carriage ready and prepared in a trice, with the top down, so that you may easily see everyone, and be seen," he promised, clearly more than eager to do as Georgina had asked. "Hyde Park will be glad to welcome us, I am sure."

Georgina smiled back at him.

"I look forward to our drive together, Lord Stratham," she murmured, just as the door closed. "In more ways than one."

CHAPTER EIGHT

This was not a wise idea.

Lady Georgina was sitting opposite Frederick with a keen look in her eye that unsettled him somewhat. He had been glad to call on her, eager to make certain that she was quite recovered, but he had not expected her to be so keen to discuss what had occurred. He was quite certain that this was her intention, given the way that she was now encouraging Lady Kingham to step out into the park for a short while, so that she might converse with her friends.

"I have been speaking to my acquaintances for some time, Mama," Lady Georgina said, firmly. "I have been speaking to them from the carriage and can continue to do so without any difficulty. With the top down like this, you will remain in full sight of me, will you not?" She smiled and tilted her head. "Therefore, there is nothing improper about you stepping out for a time."

Frederick cleared his throat, thinking that perhaps he ought to do so also.

"If it would please you, I can also make my way into the

park for a time," he said, catching Lady Georgina's sudden frown but choosing to ignore it for the time being. "I should not like to inconvenience you in any way, Lady Kingham."

The lady sighed and waved a hand.

"Forgive my demanding daughter, Lord Stratham," she said, throwing a hard look at Lady Georgina. "You have already been *so* obliging and I should not wish to take advantage of that."

Frederick sighed inwardly and forced a smile. Quite frankly, he did not want to step out of his carriage and be amongst the *ton*, for they would all be watching him rather more keenly than they were at present and, no doubt, at least one person would come to speak to him in the hope of gaining a tidbit of information which they might then use to spread even more gossip. He could almost imagine what they would be saying – how could a lady such as Lady Georgina, who was refined, beautiful, and a diamond of the first water, be in such intimate company with someone as damaged as he? His stomach tightened, but he rose from his seat and gestured for his footman to open the door.

"But of course," he said, aware of how Lady Georgina was now attempting to pin him with her gaze and choosing to ignore it entirely. "I will remain nearby, of course."

He did just as he had said and, hearing Lady Kingham leave the carriage also, clasped his hands behind his back and let himself survey the growing crowd which seemed to fill every inch of Hyde Park. He did not move to speak to anyone, glad to remain quite silent and alone for the present, and praying that no one would come to him in return.

"Lord Stratham, will you stop being so foolish?"

Frederick glanced up in surprise, seeing Lady Georgina look down at him from the carriage. Her eyes were narrowed, her lips pulled tight, and color was pouring into her cheeks.

"Lady Georgina," he replied, a little quietly, turning to face her a little more fully. "Is there something wrong?"

She let out a little huff of exasperation.

"You know very well that I am keen to speak to you alone, Lord Stratham," she said, firmly. "I will not be coy and pretend that you are unaware of the reason for my eagerness." One brow lifted. "My mother has left the carriage and there would be nothing at all improper in it, if you join me once more, given that she is only a few feet away and that we would be in her view without any difficulty, this being an open top carriage."

Shaking his head, Frederick spread his hands.

"Lady Georgina, I do not think that there is anything to discuss," he stated, knowing full well that this was not the truth of the matter, for it was quite reasonable for Lady Georgina to want to talk about what had taken place during that terrible afternoon but, at the same time, Frederick did not want to say anything more about it, given its sensitive nature. The last thing which was required was for a young lady, such as Lady Georgina, to be brought into the affair!

"Lord Stratham." Lady Georgina drew in a deep breath, still speaking from inside the carriage. "Lord Stratham, it will not come as a surprise to you that I have struggled immensely to understand all that took place. However, during my many thoughts and the *great* deal of upset that has followed, I have come to realize that me being pulled from the carriage just outside your townhouse was not merely an act of fate. Instead," she continued, "it was by design."

Frederick's stomach twisted but he kept his face impassive.

"Lady Georgina, such thoughts do not need to trouble you," he said, as gently as he could. "What occurred was terrible, and I am only glad that you are safe. You must consider your recovery and–"

"Lord Stratham, if you do not step back into this carriage immediately, then I shall be forced to take measures which will cause you a great deal of discomfiture," Lady Georgina interrupted loudly, clearly growing exasperated with his lack of willingness to do as she asked. "And do not think that I do not mean it, Lord Stratham, for if you know anything about my character, it is that I am inclined towards not doing as I ought." Her eyes narrowed even more. "Also recall that I have stated on occasion that I have found the current Season – such as it is – rather dull." One eyebrow lifted. "Mayhap I would do anything I could to enliven it." A stone dropped into Frederick's stomach as he looked into Lady Georgina's eyes. He was not used to being manipulated and the truth was, he did not like it. "I do not want to upset you or make you think ill of me, Lord Stratham," Lady Georgina finished, her tone a little gentler now, as though she could see what he was thinking. "But I must know the truth of it." One shoulder lifted in a half shrug. "I think that I deserve to know the truth, given that I was the one injured by that scoundrel. Do you not agree?"

It was this remark that convinced Frederick, rather than her attempt to force his hand. With a heavy sigh, he closed his eyes and drew in a long breath.

"I will tell you some of what occurred, Lady Georgina," he said, seeing the brightness leap into her features as she smiled down at him. "But not all. It is not necessary for you to know the depths of it, but what occurred can be a little better explained." He arched one eyebrow. "But you will not demand anything more of me."

He continued to study her face, still feeling a little discomfited by how she had tried to sway him and, at the same time, wondering what it was she had intended to do!

"Yes, of course," Lady Georgina replied, still beaming at him. "Thank you, Lord Stratham." She said nothing more until he had returned to the carriage, sitting down opposite her and at the other side of the carriage also, so that there would not be any contrived closeness between them, should someone be watching. Sitting back against the squabs, he tilted his head just a fraction and observed Lady Georgina keenly. She was a sharp-minded creature, he realized, and he would not be able to hide much from her.

"So," Lady Georgina said, her hands now clasped tightly in her lap, the only sign betraying the tension which must, by now, be coursing through her. "The fellow who attacked me, who pulled me from my carriage and threw me into your arms." Her eyes softened for a moment. "Might you know who it was?"

"I do not," Frederick answered, honestly. "I do not know his name nor where he has come from, but the Duke of Abernyte chased after him, as you know. We have every hope of knowing his name very soon. After he abandoned your carriage, the Duke's men followed him on foot."

Lady Georgina pressed her lips together, her eyes searching his face as though she wanted to make certain that he was telling the truth.

"Why was he running from you?" she asked, "What had he done?"

Frederick took a breath and considered carefully what he would say. It took some moments for him to reply and, as each second passed, he became more and more aware of Lady Georgina's scrutiny.

"He was keeping watch on Lord Brinsworth, I believe,"

he said, cautiously. "Both the Duke of Abernyte and myself have recently been in company with Lord Brinsworth and, at the time, he was within my townhouse."

"Then how did you know that man was watching all of you?" Lady Georgina asked, her brow furrowing for a moment. "Did you have a servant watching for him?"

"I did," Frederick replied, thinking that this would be the easiest explanation. "We had been aware of someone following Lord Brinsworth for a few days and wanted to make quite certain that, should he be discovered again, we would be able to capture him and demand to know why he was doing so."

Lady Georgina nodded slowly.

"And you have no reason to be suspicious of anyone in society at present?" she asked, as Frederick's stomach twisted uncomfortably. "You have no thought as to *why* Lord Brinsworth might be being followed at the moment?"

She kept her gaze fixed to his, as though she were sifting out the lies from what was in his mind, to discover the truth – but it was to no avail. Frederick shook his head.

"There is no reason to discuss such things with you, Lady Georgina," he answered, softly. "Pray do not think that I am keeping such things to myself for my own purposes, but rather understand that it is for your own safety that I do so."

This did not satisfy the lady, however, just as Frederick had expected. A scowl formed across her beautiful face.

"Lord Stratham, *please* do not leave me to question all the more!" she exclaimed, leaning forward in the carriage in her eagerness. "Something is occurring which I have become a part of and –"

"You have not become a part of it, Lady Georgina," Frederick refuted, immediately. "Please understand, what happened to you was most unfortunate and I am so very glad that we were able to take care of both you, your maid, and the carriage... when it was eventually recovered." He winced, recalling the exhausted horses, the shaken coachman, and the carriage which had lost a wheel in what had been a disastrous collision. No one had been severely hurt but the fellow within the carriage, the one who had been forcing the coachman at gunpoint to go at such a ridiculous speed, and in such a dangerous fashion, had escaped without any difficulty. The Duke's men had been too far behind to easily follow. Even now, that thought upset Frederick more than he wanted to admit. "But there cannot be more said, Lady Georgina, as much as you might wish it. It is too dangerous a situation and I would not bring you into it, not for all the world."

Lady Georgina did not fling back a response or begin to beg him outright to tell her all, as he had expected. Instead, she sat back in her seat once more and considered him carefully. For some minutes, nothing more was said. Frederick could hear only the laughter and hubbub of conversation from outside the carriage as others passed by and felt himself grow a trifle uncomfortable as her silence dragged on. He had not expected this from Lady Georgina, had not thought that she would consider things in such a careful manner. And yet it seemed that was precisely what she was doing.

"I understand, Lord Stratham." Lady Georgina's voice was soft and her expression gentle. "You are trying to protect me."

"Yes." Frederick let out a breath of relief. "Yes, Lady Georgina, that is precisely what I am trying to do."

"And that is honorable," came the reply. "Although I must ask you something more – pray, do not fear that it will be to demand more from you, for that will not be what I ask." One hand had lifted towards him, palm upwards as she saw his hesitancy. "If this man, this ruffian, saw my face and knows the carriage which he took to be my father's – for all of society is speaking of it and I hardly think that it would be difficult to find out, should he wish to – then is there not a little concern in that regard?"

A deep frown pulled at Frederick's brow.

"What do you mean?"

"Well..." She shrugged one shoulder, looking back at him carefully. "If this man knows who I am and, given that I have seen his face and know exactly what he looks like, should I worry that he might now return to make certain that I do not speak of him to any other?" She did not smile and there was no gleam in her eye which spoke of a sense of triumph. Instead, she appeared to be a little pale, for her cheeks held no color and even her blue eyes seemed to have dimmed. "He knows that I am the daughter of Lord Kingham and, given that men are pursuing him – men that I am acquainted with – then there must now be a concern that he might return to make certain of my silence." She shuddered violently and Frederick leaned forward in concern, quickly realizing what she meant, and cursing himself for not thinking of it himself. "This is my first outing in society since the attack and mayhap..." She closed her eyes. "Mayhap he has been waiting to make certain that I can return to society rather than lingering on at home, kept asleep by laudanum until my injuries improve. After all, he would not have any knowledge as to my present state."

"No, indeed not." Frederick shook his head and ran one hand down his face, upset with himself that he had not even considered such a thing before. He had been correct in his assessment of Lady Georgina – she had a sharp mind and had overtaken him in terms of his judgment in this matter. A little embarrassed, he cleared his throat and looked back at her. "You are correct, Lady Georgina," he said, quietly. "I confess that I had not thought of such a concern, but it is there, and it is apparent now that you have spoken it, and I am sorry that I had given it not even a modicum of thought." Instinctively, he reached out and took her hand, grateful when she grasped his tightly. "Lady Georgina, I have been foolish in this matter. I have been so busy thinking about how to capture this fellow, as well as worrying about your wellbeing that I did not even think to ask you about what you had seen. Nor did I imagine that the man responsible for stealing your father's carriage might, thereafter, then consider returning to find you, for fear that you would speak of him to us!" Grimacing, he shook his head, his fingers tightening on hers. "Forgive me."

"There is nothing to forgive," she answered swiftly, returning the pressure of his hand with a press of her own. "Lord Stratham, I was wrong to try to force your hand when it came to telling me the truth of what had occurred." As Frederick looked into her face, he saw Lady Georgina swallow hard, perhaps finally realizing the real seriousness of what she had stumbled into. "It is I who ought to be seeking *your* forgiveness. I am a little brash at times and certainly demanding, but I ought not to have done such a thing in this matter. Forgive me, Lord Stratham."

Frederick's heart lifted and he gave her a small smile.

"Thank you, Lady Georgina," he answered, not wanting to pretend that what she had done had sat well with him. He appreciated her apology and her consideration of her behavior greatly, for it showed an awareness of herself and her faults which, Frederick had to admit, he admired. "Would that I could explain more but..." He glanced out of the window and saw Lady Kingham wave one hand in her friend's direction, making him believe that she would soon return to them both. There was not much time remaining. "Permit me this, Lady Georgina." Shifting in his seat a little more, he reached out so that he grasped both of her hands in both of his, looking firmly into her eyes so that she might see only him and not become distracted by anything else. He wanted her to listen to every single word that he had to say and to understand the promise he was about to make to her. "I will, I swear to you, protect you from this man and from those he works for." He did not go into further detail but still saw the shock in her eyes. "I will return you and your mother to your townhouse and, thereafter, will make my way home and send two men to guard the house from any possible attack."

Lady Georgina blinked rapidly, her cheeks now very pale indeed.

"You have such men?"

"I do," Frederick replied, with a small, rueful smile. "It has been necessary for me to do so and whilst I will not go into further explanation, you can rest assured that they will not hesitate to intervene if necessary. There will be at least two men watching the house both day and night so that you might feel safe within the confines of your father's house." Nodding slowly, Lady Georgina closed her eyes for a moment. There was no sparkle in her eyes now, no glee in her expression nor her voice. Instead, there was a deep and almost paralyzing fear which, having only just come upon her, now seemed to have taken a strong hold. "If you would, Lady Georgina, you might send me word of which social events you plan to attend," he finished, throwing another quick look, and seeing Lady Kingham now approaching the carriage. Letting go of Lady Georgina's hands, he shifted back into his seat. "I will, of course, do all that I can to be in attendance also, but if not I, then the Duke of Abernyte or Lord Brinsworth will be there in my stead. You will be quite safe, Lady Georgina."

She nodded, her jaw working furiously for a moment as she blinked, evidently stemming the flow of tears which threatened so that her mother would not see.

"You will need to talk with me again, Lord Stratham," she said, hoarsely. "There is more that must be discussed, I assume?"

Frederick frowned.

"I do not understand –"

"You have not asked me what this fellow looks like," Lady Georgina interrupted, quickly. "I have a picture of him in my mind and can describe him without difficulty. That, I assume, will be required?"

Again, a sense of foolishness crept over Frederick, but he ignored it entirely, telling himself that he need not give any consideration to his feelings at present but rather instead, take heed of what Lady Georgina herself said.

"Yes, that is so," he agreed, quickly. "The Duke of Abernyte did not manage to see the man clearly and nor did Lord Brinsworth. Therefore, of course, we will need to talk with you so that we understand the sort of man we are searching for."

Lady Georgina nodded and the ghost of a smile pulled at her lips.

"And mayhap you might be willing to tell me a little more about this man," she said, hopefully. "I should very much like to know why I am in so much danger."

Frederick cleared his throat as the carriage door was opened for Lady Kingham to re-enter, his gaze still fixed on Lady Georgina.

"I must speak with the others but yes, Lady Georgina, I believe there is more to say," he promised, speaking in a low voice. "Be on your guard but not overwhelmed with fright. You are protected."

"And you are my protector," she replied, her expression softening suddenly as she looked back at him.

An extraordinary emotion washed over Frederick in an instant, seeming to fill him with warmth, longing, hope, and desire all in one heady moment – and it took him some time before he could pull his gaze away from her. He did not know how to explain it, or what it was precisely that he now felt, but given the look on Lady Georgina's face, she too felt something of the same.

"Ah, you have returned, Lord Stratham." Lady Kingham sat back in her seat, looking quite satisfied with herself and not at all perturbed that Frederick had been sitting in the carriage with her daughter alone. "And you, Georgina, are you quite well?" She frowned and Frederick shot a hurried glance towards the young lady, seeing still that she was quite pale but with a tiny spot of color in each cheek. "You look a little tired."

"Yes, Mama," Lady Georgina agreed, although she did not look at Frederick as she spoke. "I am quite fatigued. Indeed, I would be glad to return home, if that would suit you?"

Lady Kingham nodded.

"But of course, I am quite tired also," she agreed, as Frederick turned to signal the coachman to leave Hyde Park and return the ladies home. "You have done well, Georgina, although I do hope you are not overwhelmed by your return to society."

The carriage moved and Frederick steadied himself so that he would not bump Lady Kingham. As he did so, his eyes met Lady Georgina's, and, once more, Frederick found himself lost in a sea of emotion.

"I am a little overwhelmed, I confess," Lady Georgina replied, speaking with such quietness that Frederick strained to hear her although her eyes were fixed on his, sending an awareness through him that her words were not for Lady Kingham but him instead. "But I am quite certain that all will be well."

Her lips curved into a small smile and Frederick returned it with one of his own, glad that she had confidence in him, and feeling filled with a determination that he *would* protect her, no matter the cost. It was as Lady Georgina had said, all would be well – and he was the one who would make it so.

CHAPTER NINE

*T*here was a great swirl of nervousness that coursed through Georgina's veins every time she so much as considered stepping out of the house. She had not noticed either of the men that Lord Stratham had assured her he would send but, given the fact that she knew Lord Stratham's word could be trusted, Georgina had to believe that they were both present, as he had said.

After their drive and conversation in the carriage yesterday afternoon, Georgina had found herself in a state of disarray. Rather than finding the answers she had hoped for, and the clarity that she believed she desired, Georgina now found that she had been given rather more to fear than before. She had not realized that there was a danger lurking nearby, not until Lord Stratham had begun to explain what had taken place and now it had left her feeling very uncertain indeed.

Still, Georgina reflected, as she looked at herself in the mirror, she had nothing to fear when it came to her current circumstance. She was to go out this evening to a small soiree and, having written to Lord Stratham to inform him of it, she had then been informed that he would be in attendance also. The note had been short and direct, but it had brought Georgina a great measure of comfort, as well as a small smile to her lips when she thought of being in his company again.

I did not behave well.

Shame burned her cheeks as she recalled how she had attempted to force Lord Stratham's hand by practically demanding that he inform her of what had happened the afternoon that she had been attacked. She had not been entirely sure what she had thought to do to make him tell her everything she had hoped for and, in fact, expected – that the threat would be enough. But the change in his expression when he had looked up at her when she had said such a thing as that, had brought such a sense of mortification to her that she had known immediately that it had been the wrong thing to both say and threaten to do. She had been glad that there had been an opportunity to apologize and that he had been so very gracious in accepting that apology from her. As much as she wanted to know what was going on and why she was now in so much danger, Georgina also wanted Lord Stratham to think well of her. They had become rather close in such a short space of time and the impression Georgina made upon him would, most likely, be the lasting one.

He was very gracious. And very kind.

"And determined to protect me." Georgina spoke her last thought aloud, still looking at her reflection in the mirror and noticing how her eyes brightened as she thought of him. She had found the *ton* so very dull and was tired and bored of having the same gentlemen paraded before her and pushed into her considerations by her mother – and then, Lord Stratham had appeared. Had it not been for her mother's lack of eagerness to acquaint herself with him, Georgina might never have taken such an interest in the gentleman, but she was glad that she had done. There was a warmth in their acquaintance now – and a great deal of respect on her part, at least.

And perhaps something more?

A blush caught her cheeks and Georgina looked away from her reflection, rising to her feet and self-consciously smoothing her gown. She did not want to think of what else she was feeling at present, as regarded Lord Stratham. Whilst it was something that she would allow to grow and flourish, if it intended to do so, there was no great need for Georgina to consider it deeply at present. Besides which, if she felt something more for Lord Stratham than he felt for her, then would it not lead to heartbreak? She had to be wise and cautious and explore these new emotions with great care.

"Georgina."

Georgina turned swiftly, seeing her mother framed in the doorway.

"Yes, Mama?"

"Are you quite ready?" Her mother's lips were tight. "We have been waiting below stairs for ten minutes! I have already sent up two maids to fetch you and whilst both stated that you were dressed and prepared, you said that you would be with us in only a few moments! And now–," she broke off, gesturing wildly towards Georgina, "I have been forced to come up to find you myself and see that there is nothing hindering you whatsoever!"

Aware that she had been doing nothing other than letting her thoughts cloud her mind, Georgina dropped her head, a little ashamed.

"I am sorry, Mama," she said, softly. "Forgive me. I am,

perhaps, a little reluctant to step out this evening."

That was true enough, for Georgina knew that most of the guests present this evening would be aware of her presence and would, most likely, seek to speak and gossip about her and what had occurred. News about the dramatic affair had reached the ears of practically everyone in society and Georgina knew that she could well be the center of attention.

"My dear." There was more sympathy in Lady Kingham's voice than Georgina had expected and, as she looked up, she was all the more astonished to see her mother coming closer, reaching out to take Georgina's hands. "I am so very sorry for my lack of consideration, my dear girl," she continued, as Georgina blinked in amazement. "You must be quite anxious but pray, have no concern." She smiled and Georgina tried to smile back, despite her surprise. "You will have almost *everyone* eager to speak to you! Just think of all of the gentlemen who will want to dance!" She threw a quick, worried glance down towards Georgina's feet. "You will be able to dance, I hope?"

"I – I think that I will dance only a few dances, Mama, just to make certain that I do not worsen my ankle," Georgina replied, slowly, her smile fading as she realized that her mother's eagerness and understanding came from the knowledge that Georgina would be sought out above any other when it came to this evening. "It is not painful at all, as you know, but it would be best to be cautious."

Lady Kingham tutted but waved a hand carelessly.

"Very well, very well," she said, quickly. "It will not matter, for there will be many gentlemen who will wish to converse with you so that they might know all that took place!" She pressed Georgina's hands. "You *will* speak to them, will you not?"

Georgina swallowed hard, tears beginning to form as she realized just how little her mother truly cared for her wellbeing. Yes, she had been concerned for her daughter after the accident and had been gravely anxious for her ankle, but now that Georgina was recovered, now that her ankle was healed, it seemed that Lady Kingham had resorted to her usual manner of things and thought only of the *ton* and how she might encourage Georgina into the very best of matches.

"I will try, Mama," she answered, a little throatily. "Lord Stratham will be there also, and I am certain that—"

"Trust me, my dear Georgina, there will be many gentlemen there who are a good deal more suitable than Lord Stratham," Lady Kingham interrupted, leading Georgina from the room. "Yes, I am aware that he is a Marquess and that he has done a great deal to protect and support you, but he is still a gentleman with marked features, and can you imagine what the *ton* would say if he was seen to be *courting* you!" She shook her head briskly, going against all that both Georgina and Lord Kingham had said about Lord Stratham and how he was to be encouraged as an acquaintance, should Georgina wish it. "There will be Marquesses aplenty seeking you out, I am sure of it. And they will be all more handsome than he!"

Georgina wrenched her arm from her mother's, turning on her swiftly. A torrent of hot anger poured into her veins as she glared at Lady Kingham, her eyes narrowing. She would not allow her mother to speak of Lord Stratham in such a way, not just because he had come to her aid, but also because of just how much he had come to mean to Georgina herself.

"That is enough, Mama!" Georgina's voice rang out into the hallway, catching the attention of Lord Kingham, who was standing waiting for them both by the front door. "I hold Lord Stratham in high regard! I think him kind, genteel and, quite frankly, very handsome indeed. I care nothing for his 'marked features' as you so call it, but instead think it extremely poor of *you* to place such weight upon it! This evening, I expect to be in Lord Stratham's company a great deal." She lifted her chin, taking in her mother's now rather pale face, from which two angry eyes blazed. "In fact, should he ask to court me, then I have every intention of accepting him without hesitation! Now, shall we depart?"

She spun on her heel and marched off, down the stairs and to the door, walking past her father who stood in evident amazement at this particular display. Georgina cared nothing for the hysterics which were soon to follow, no doubt, for she had made her position quite clear and was glad of it. Nothing her mother said about Lord Stratham would be allowed to pass Georgina by, for he was worth defending.

And she had meant every word she had said.

"Good evening, Lady Georgina."

Georgina sighed inwardly but kept her smile fixed in place. It would not do to anger her mother further this evening. Thankfully, Lord Kingham had smoothed things between them as the carriage had taken them to Lord Hensley's ball, but Georgina knew that even a momentary slip on her part could send her mother back into a flurry of upset and anger.

"Good evening, Lord Jeffries." She shot a glance at her mother who was, Georgina noted, looking steadily elsewhere, as though she wanted to allow Lord Jeffries full command of Georgina's attention. "You are enjoying the ball, I hope?"

Lord Jeffries chuckled, his eyes gleaming in a most disagreeable manner.

"Not as much as you are, I am certain!" he exclaimed, reaching forward to pat her arm for a moment. "You have almost everyone present seeking out your company!"

Georgina's smile slipped.

"It is not a matter I wish to discuss, however," she replied, tightly. "In fact, Lord Jeffries, I would appreciate it if you did not ask me a single thing about what occurred. As I have just expressed, it caused me great pain and struggle and it is not something which I would like to bring to mind again."

"Oh, but how can you say so?" Lord Jeffries cried, expressing once more to her just how little he considered her – or, indeed, anyone other than himself. "All of society wishes to hear what you have endured! It should be an honor – nay, a delight - to speak of it all when you are enjoying such fame!"

"And yet, I am still quite reluctant to do so," Georgina replied, firmly, turning her head away and silently praying that there would soon come another to whom she might speak. "Lord Jeffries, I –"

"Good evening, Lady Georgina."

It was with both relief and a swell of great emotion that Georgina turned to speak to Lord Stratham who had appeared as though in answer to her silent plea.

"Lord Stratham," she breathed, her shoulders slumping in relief. "How *very* good to see you."

Realizing what she had just said, and precisely how she had said it, Georgina threw one horrified glance towards her mother, only to see her caught up in conversation with Lady

Kellingston. Lady Matilda must be present also, although Georgina had not yet had the opportunity to speak to her.

"Are you dancing this evening, Lady Georgina?" Lord Stratham asked pleasantly, ignoring Lord Jeffries who was looking a little disgruntled that he had been so interrupted. "I would quite understand if you chose not to do so, however."

"That is *precisely* what I was about to ask."

Before Georgina could say or do anything, Lord Jeffries had reached forward and grasped her dance card, hauling it towards him. Because it was still slipped around her wrist, Georgina found her hand being pulled upwards and rather hard too, making her let out an exclamation as she was tugged forward.

"Lord Jeffries!"

Lord Stratham was there in a moment, his hand pressing down on Lord Jeffries', his brow low and a determination in his expression which forced Lord Jeffries to respond.

"Lord Jeffries! Unhand my daughter at once!"

It took a few moments for Georgina to be freed from Lord Jeffries' demanding grasp but, eventually, she was set free. Her mother, having heard Georgina's cry, now stood with both hands on her hips, glaring furiously at the gentleman she had, at one time, been so eager to press into Georgina's affections.

"I thought only to dance with Lady Georgina," Lord Jeffries stated, sounding a trifle plaintive as he looked from Lady Kingham to Georgina and then to Lady Kellingston and finally to Lord Stratham. "After all, I was here speaking to her first before Lord Stratham and –"

"That does not give you leave to simply grasp my dance card and pull me towards you in such an uncouth manner!"

Georgina exclaimed, rubbing her wrist gently. "And had you any concern, Lord Jeffries, you would know that my ankle is still a little tender and that I had thought only to dance a few this evening." Her chin lifted. "I do not think I have any dances remaining which might be given to you."

Lady Kingham sniffed, her eyes narrowing.

"I quite agree, Georgina," she stated, coming to the defense of her daughter and her reputation. "Do excuse us, Lord Jeffries, but Georgina will be unable to stand up with you this evening." It took a few moments but, eventually, Lord Jeffries – muttering under his breath – turned away from them and left them all to stand together. Georgina let out a small sigh of relief, shaking her head as she looked down at the red mark which the ribbon had left on her skin. "Are you quite all right, Georgina?"

She looked up at her mother.

"Yes, I am quite well, Mama," she answered, only for Lady Kingham to then turn to Lord Stratham.

"It seems I am to thank you once more for rescuing my daughter, Lord Stratham," she said, her voice a little tight. "Lord Jeffries was... inappropriate in his manner. Thank you for stepping in and making certain that Georgina did not come to any further harm."

Lord Stratham bowed.

"But of course," he replied, as Georgina smiled back at him. "Lady Georgina, if you are not to dance, might you wish for a short turn about the room?" He looked directly at Lady Kingham. "We would, of course, not go far from you, Lady Kingham."

Georgina shot an inquiring glance towards her mother, hoping that Lady Kingham would agree and, after only a few moments of hesitation, the agreement came. Relieved that she would not have to linger next to her mother and continue to speak to gentlemen and ladies who wanted nothing more than to hear the very intricate details of what had occurred, Georgina accepted Lord Stratham's arm, and together, they stepped away from her mother and Lady Kellingston.

"You have saved me in more ways than one, Lord Stratham," Georgina murmured, as he smiled down at her. "I have had nothing other than question after question about what I endured and what happened and who was there and what injuries I sustained…" She rolled her eyes and laughed wryly. "It has been very tedious indeed."

"But I thought the whole thing had served to enliven your presence here in London somewhat," Lord Stratham retorted, teasingly. "Had you not said just how dull you found the place?"

"I do not say so now!" Georgina replied, laughing. Her smile died away as she looked into Lord Stratham's face. They kept to the side of the ballroom, where the presence of others nearby was less and the shadows a little thicker so that they were not so easily seen. Georgina felt a heaviness on her heart as she saw the seriousness in his eyes and knew that she was still in the midst of something very significant indeed. "Has there been any sign of the man who stole my father's carriage?" she asked, as Lord Stratham shook his head. "What of anyone drawing near to the townhouse, in the hope of finding me?"

Lord Stratham did not instantly shake his head and Georgina caught her breath, one hand pressed against her stomach lightly.

"There was someone," Lord Stratham murmured, quietly, "but the men I stationed there were easily able to intercept him." He reached across and pressed her hand as it rested on his other arm. "You need not fear, Lady

Georgina. I said I would protect you, and I have every intention of doing so."

Georgina nodded, ignoring the swirling fear which attempted to take hold of her.

"I would not lie to you," Lord Stratham said, gently. "But nor do I want to worry you unnecessarily."

Trying to smile, Georgina looked up at him.

"I would rather know the truth of it that remain blissfully ignorant," she answered. "I presume that you would now like to know what the man I saw looked like?"

Seeing Lord Stratham nod, Georgina quickly drew to mind the man who had jumped into her carriage so unexpectedly. In a low voice, she told Lord Stratham everything about him that she remembered, knowing that he was listening intently to every single word she said.

"You have done well to recall so much, Lady Georgina," Lord Stratham murmured, making Georgina smile. "That will be extremely helpful.

"And will you tell me *why* he was pursuing Lord Brinsworth?" Georgina asked, a little hopefully. "If you do not wish to, then I will not ask again, for I do not want to force you into doing so."

Lord Stratham stopped walking, turned to face her, and held her gaze for some moments. Georgina said nothing, looking back at him and wondering silently if he would consider her trustworthy or strong enough to hear the truth from him.

"It...." Lord Stratham closed his eyes and shook his head. "It is to do with our war against France and Napoleon's forces," he said, opening his eyes again to look at her. "The Duke of Abernyte's efforts have been well known amongst society for some time, whereas both myself and Lord Brinsworth, have been sent back to England due to injuries sustained during battle." His lips twisted as he lifted one hand towards his face in a frustrated gesture. "I would have remained, but the choice was not one that was given to me."

Georgina did not immediately answer. Her mind was trying to work through what Lord Stratham had said, trying to understand what he meant by talking of the war effort whilst being here in the middle of London. Her heart began to pound furiously as she slowly began to realize what he was suggesting.

"You – you mean to say that some of the French are here in London?" she asked, as Lord Stratham's lips pulled tight. "That they are here to seek out... those in high positions? Those who have returned from war?"

"They seek to invade us," Lord Stratham said frankly, causing Georgina to gasp in horror. "And what is worse, there are those in England itself who seek to help them."

She could not answer him for a moment, such was her shock. Her breathing was ragged, her stomach tight with the shock of what she had heard. Lord Stratham was suggesting – no, *telling* her that there were those in the *ton* who sought to help their enemy.

"And you..." She closed her eyes, steadying herself inwardly. "You seek to find out those who do such things?"

Lord Stratham nodded.

"I do," he answered, as she looked at him again, seeing the honesty in his expression and knowing in her heart that he spoke every word of truth. "There are three of us at present doing so – and whilst we believed that our true purposes here in London were hidden from the enemy, it now seems that we were mistaken." He grimaced. "Someone has followed Lord Brinsworth, clearly suspicious that he has come to London to meet with the Duke of

Abernyte. And they have succeeded in discovering the truth, for he has been seen meeting with both myself and the Duke on two separate occasions." Looking away, he let out a long, heavy breath. "Our meetings were necessary, else we would not have done such a thing. But we have to know who we are considering and what we must do next – letters and the like would not suffice. Besides which," he finished, grimly, "I have no doubt that it would have been noted by our enemy that many notes were going between our three houses."

"Good gracious."

Georgina kept her hand pressed against her stomach, feeling a little dizzy as she took in all that the Marquess had said. How could it be that someone within the *ton* could behave in such a treacherous manner? She could hardly believe it, could hardly take it in and yet she knew, without any hesitation whatsoever, that everything Lord Stratham had told her was true.

"I should not have told you all of this," Lord Stratham murmured, looking at her steadily, his brows furrowing. "It is too much for you. I –"

"It is not too much." Georgina grasped his hand tightly, looking back into his eyes with a steadiness she did not feel. "I am grateful for your trust, Lord Stratham."

He pressed his lips together but did not answer her, returning the pressure of her fingers.

"Therefore, the man you were chasing – the man who stole my carriage – was someone involved with the French," Georgina confirmed aloud, as Lord Stratham nodded. "Do you believe that he is one of the *ton*?"

"No." Lord Stratham shook his head. "It will have been someone working at the behest of his master. That is why we must discover him, for we have nothing other than him, aside from our other single piece of information." Shrugging one shoulder, he looked away. "And that is why we must protect you also, Lady Georgina," he finished. "It is not only that they might come to seek you out for fear that you will tell us of what you saw, but also that there is now a connection between us that could be used ill." Slowly, his eyes lifted back to hers as if he feared to look into her eyes steadfastly, for fear of what he might see there. "I am sorry for that. I did not mean for you to ever become involved in this affair. It was most unfortunate that your carriage slowed directly outside my townhouse at the time that this... this *scoundrel* sought to escape us, but as it stands, there is nothing that can be done to change that. No doubt whoever was watching and directing that fellow is all too aware of the connection between us. I would hate for them to use you ill, simply to force my hand."

This did not come as a great shock to Georgina, possibly because she had already felt so much astonishment and horror that she could not feel anything more. Instead, she simply nodded solemnly, aware that he still held her hands.

"It is not your doing, Lord Stratham," she said, softly. "It is I who introduced myself to you, was it not? And my carriage was simply taking me for a drive, happening to stop in the exact spot where that fellow might climb inside. None of this is your fault, Lord Stratham and I–"

Georgina stopped dead as Lord Stratham held up one hand, his eyes closing tightly as an expression of guilt came into his face. His cheeks were a little flushed, his brows knotted together, and his head dropped forward. Her stomach flipped itself upside down and Georgina dropped Lord Stratham's hand.

"What is it?" she asked, her hands clasping tightly together as she looked into Lord Stratham's face, feeling herself grow hot and clammy as she waited for him to respond. "Lord Stratham, what is wrong?"

He shook his head, his jaw working tightly for a moment.

"I cannot explain – *will* not explain all to you, Lady Georgina," he began, his words short and punctuated like shots from a gun. "But had you not introduced yourself to me, then I would have made certain to achieve an introduction myself. I had reason to become acquainted with you, a reason that I cannot express. But," he continued, eagerly, his head lifting, "I have found our acquaintance so *very* delightful that I have never found myself thinking of ending it, once my task is completed. Indeed, I have found myself drawn to you, caught up in affection for you, and finding that, despite my own struggles and trials, I have looked to you and found something more within my heart, something that I have not felt before. Pray, Lady Georgina, do not think ill of me, for there was never any malice in my intentions."

Her heart dropped to the floor and refused to be pulled up again.

"You – you wanted to use me as a particular connection?" she asked, her voice rasping hoarsely. "Simply for your own endeavors?"

"For the safety and protection of King and country," Lord Stratham replied, quickly. "Pray understand, Lady Georgina, it was not a personal decision. It was one that I had no other choice but to pursue and –"

Georgina held up one hand, silencing him midway through his speech.

"Lord Stratham, I should return to my mother." Her heart was heavy and sore, her mind weighed down with all manner of thoughts. "Pray return me to her."

Lord Stratham's face fell, and he closed his eyes tightly, screwing them up in evident frustration.

"Lady Georgina, please."

"No." She shook her head firmly and then turned on her heel. "My mother, if you please."

It took but a moment for Lord Stratham to do as she had asked. Coming to walk beside her, but without offering her his arm – Georgina would not have taken it even if he *had* done so – they began to walk together back towards Lady Kingham. Georgina's vision threatened to be overcome with tears, but she forced them back quickly, refusing to permit herself to be so affected. There was a great deal in what Lord Stratham had said and Georgina needed time to consider it all, to allow herself the opportunity to catch her breath and think on the implications. She could not do so now, not when he stood her beside her, not when he was so very near to her.

"What was that other piece of information you spoke of?"

She rounded on him suddenly, making Lord Stratham blink in surprise.

"I beg your pardon?"

"You said only a few minutes ago that there was nothing other than my description of that ruffian, save for another single piece of information." Her eyes narrowed, her heart beating painfully as her fingers curled up into fists, her whole body tense. "What was it?"

Lord Stratham's brows knotted together.

"I do not think that this is something you need know of, Lady Georgina. It is not that I wish to keep it from you deliberately – I do not wish to keep it from you for my grati-fication – but rather because it is of an overly sensitive nature."

Georgina lifted one eyebrow, feeling hot tears spring into her eyes once more. Her heart quailed at the truth that now settled in her heart, her mind having come to its own conclusions and needing only Lord Stratham to confirm it.

"You consider that someone close to me might be working for the French," she stated, seeing no sense of surprise or horror climb into Lord Stratham's expression. "Is that not so? That is why you wished to become acquainted with me so that you might have a better connection to that particular person. Unless," she added, her eyes flaring wide, "you thought that I..."

"No, *no!*" Lord Stratham's eyes were fixed on hers, his whole expression one of horror. "I did not even think for a *moment* that you might be involved, Lady Georgina. Pray, do not even allow yourself to think that."

Georgina let out a long, slow breath and swallowed hard, realizing that, whilst he had not admitted to what else she had said, his response to her told her that she was quite correct.

"Then who is it that you are considering, Lord Stratham?" she asked, softly.

Lord Stratham looked back into her eyes and said nothing, his own eyes a little hooded as though he feared to tell her. Georgina made to say more, to demand that he be honest with her, given all that he had admitted, only for her mother to come sailing towards her, forcing them apart.

"Georgina, you *must* come and speak to Lord Bulford," she exclaimed, ignoring Lord Stratham entirely. "Did you know that he is courting Lady Matilda?"

She laughed and pressed Georgina's hand, bearing her away, her laughter quite brash against the tumult which was going on in Georgina's heart. She did not so much as glance at Lord Stratham as she moved away, finding herself almost relieved to be gone from his company. Everything around her seemed to slow as her mother led her to where Lady Matilda and Lord Bulford stood, the sounds of laughter and conversation seeming dull, the music out of tune. She could not even force a smile and, as Lady Kingham made the introductions, it took all of Georgina's strength to drop into a curtsey. Dazed and upset, she allowed her mother, Lady Matilda, Lord Bulford, and Lady Kellingston to talk, standing there as a silent observer as she fought to consider everything of the new information that had been given to her.

Her heart was quite broken and filled with sorrow over the realization that Lord Stratham's connection with her had been for reasons of his own. Yes, he had spoken about what had come thereafter, but Georgina was not certain that she could trust what he had said. What if it had been spoken merely as a way to keep her close to him, to keep her near so that he might continue to pursue whoever it was he wanted to seek out?

"Georgina?"

Georgina looked up sharply, seeing how Lady Matilda was studying her, a small frown creasing her brow.

"Forgive me," she said, trying to put together a façade which could be believed. "I had a small twinge in my ankle, that is all."

She smiled at Lady Matilda, who, in turn, smiled back – albeit rather tentatively. The conversation continued, and Georgina forced herself to pay attention, not wanting to upset or confuse her friend any more than she already had done. Lord Stratham, for the time being, would have to be gone from her mind. When it was quiet, when she was alone, *then* would be the time to allow everything she had heard and everything she felt to come to the fore.

CHAPTER TEN

"Stratham."

Frederick walked into the Duke of Abernyte's drawing room and threw himself into a chair, a huff of breath escaping him. The Duke's brow lifted.

"Brandy?"

"Please." Frederick held out his hand as the Duke handed him a glass. "Thank you."

Lord Brinsworth, who had been sitting opposite Frederick, rose.

"Another for me, I think," he murmured, taking his empty glass towards the decanter. "Something, it seems, has not gone well." He threw a glance towards Frederick. "Is Lady Georgina quite well?"

Frederick nodded, a tight band about his chest.

"I told her everything."

The Duke of Abernyte and Lord Brinsworth both froze in position, their eyes suddenly snapping to Frederick.

"I could not keep it from her," Frederick continued, staring at the glowing embers in the fireplace. "Some of the things she said were..." He closed his eyes, recalling how

Lady Georgina had been so very eager to make certain that he neither took nor felt any blame or guilt. "I did not say specifically that we were considering her father, but I do not think it will take long for her to realize it."

Lord Brinsworth shook his head.

"You have come to care for the lady," he muttered, darkly. "That was foolish."

Bristling, Frederick glared at him.

"It is not something that one can predict!" he exclaimed, as the Duke listened carefully, without making a single remark. "I did not think that I would come to care for any young lady, given that my mind is full of the dire situation we find ourselves in at present, but these last days I have found myself struggling to think of anything but her."

Grimacing, Lord Brinsworth lifted his glass in Frederick's direction.

"Then you have permitted yourself to become distracted," he stated, as though Frederick was in some way in the wrong for feeling as he did. "How can you do your duty if you are thinking only of the lady?"

Resisting the urge to throw himself out of his chair, stride across the room and grasp Lord Brinsworth by the collar, Frederick contented himself with a scowl.

"You will know what I speak of one day, Brinsworth," he muttered, furiously. "Then we will see whether you find it as easy as you state simply to stop thinking of the lady."

Lord Brinsworth made to reply but the Duke stepped between them, clearly eager for there not to be an argument.

"Enough, gentlemen," he said, sharply, "else I fear that you will come to blows!" He grimaced, looking hard at Frederick. "You thought it wise to tell Lady Georgina everything?"

Frederick closed his eyes, sinking back into his chair.

"I do not know if it was wise," he admitted, thinking that he had perhaps made an error in judgment when he had spoken so freely. "But it is done. Lady Georgina is well otherwise, although she was perturbed when I spoke of the man who had attempted to gain access to her house through the servants' quarters." He had not gone into particular detail in that regard with the lady, but he had seen the fright in her expression regardless. "My men will continue to remain posted there, of course. However, Lady Georgina gave me a very thorough description of the man who attacked her in the carriage."

"Oh?" Lord Brinsworth sat back down in his chair, albeit with a reluctance that was more than apparent, given the scowl that he shot in the Duke's direction. "What did she say?"

Frederick quickly told them both everything that the lady had said, although the words did not come without pain. He could still recall Lady Georgina's face as she had spoken, so eager to help and so willing to do what she could. He felt as though he had betrayed her trust but, at the same time, was glad that he had told her the truth, despite the consequences which had followed.

"Well, that is of help, at least," the Duke murmured, still casting a sharp eye over both Frederick and Lord Brinsworth as though he expected them to jump up suddenly and come to blows. "In addition, the conclusion we have come to is that there is no other gentleman bearing the name required within London, who remains a possibility after our investigations so far, save for Lord Kingham." He frowned and looked hard at Frederick. "That does mean that—"

"Yes, I am aware of what that could mean," Frederick

stated, firmly. "You need not concern yourself in that regard, I know what Lady Georgina might come to suffer."

Lord Brinsworth frowned.

"You are certain that we are not missing anyone else?"

The Duke shook his head.

"Not unless the gentleman in question has returned to Bath," he said, shrugging. "Or to his estate. There is one other gentleman I had thought of – Lord Kellingston." Frederick's ears pricked up. He knew that name. "But he is at war," the Duke continued, his lips twisting. "So I highly doubt that it is *he* who has been communicating with the enemy here in England."

"I have heard of Kellingston," Frederick murmured, tilting his head to the left as he tried to recall where he had heard that title before. "There must be someone here in London who bears it." His frown grew steadily until, with a sudden flash, it came to him. "Ah, his mother and sister!" he exclaimed, recalling how the Lady had spoken to him some time ago and introduced Lady Matilda. "Lady Kellingston is in London with her daughter, Lady Matilda. Lady Matilda is, in fact, a good friend of Lady Georgina, from what I understand."

This was not, of course, of any significance but it still explained where Frederick knew the title from.

"Then it appears as though Lord Kingham is the gentleman we seek," Lord Brinsworth replied, swirling his brandy. "The one who has been passing on information to our enemy, who has been helping to injure those most significant to the Crown." He sent a knowing look in the Duke's direction. "And someone who is attempting to do all they can to aid the French attempt at invasion."

"He did know more about me than I expected," Frederick agreed, reluctantly. "Lady Georgina spoke of what she had been told by her father, which did make me wonder how he had come to know of such particulars, given that he is not a gentleman who often frequents society events." He shrugged. "It may have been through an entirely innocent means but, given that you have both found your acquaintances with a title that might fit to be without fault, then I suppose we must consider him."

The Duke nodded, although there was a faint expression of concern on his features.

"Will you be able to continue your acquaintance with Lady Georgina to the point that you might be able to ascertain the truth with surety?" he asked, sounding a little doubtful. "If she has become so very upset, then is there not a concern that she will no longer be willing to be in your company?"

Frederick's heart twisted painfully, and he threw back his brandy before he answered.

"There is a chance that she may behave in such a way," he admitted. "I will do what I can."

"Then what is our plan?" Lord Brinsworth asked, sitting forward in his chair with an eagerness that Frederick had not seen before. "We cannot just sit about and wait for Lord Kingham to do something which would prove whether or not he is the one we have been looking for." He turned to Frederick and arched one eyebrow. "What can be done?"

Frederick hesitated, then lifted one shoulder.

"I could mention something in his presence and see if it brought anything about?" he said, slowly. "For example, if I was to state – perhaps, accidentally – that I am to meet with someone on a particular matter regarding the war, then if someone else were to join us, someone with dark intentions, then we would know that Lord Kingham was the one to share it."

It was only the very bare bones of a plan, but it was better than nothing.

"Yes, I see what you mean," the Duke said slowly, his eyes thoughtful. "That would be a good idea. It would have to appear as though it were a slip of the tongue, however, Stratham. You would be able to do that?"

Nodding, Frederick felt his stomach twist as he thought of how he would explain himself to Lady Georgina, should it prove to be true that Lord Kingham was working for the French.

"I will find a way, I am quite capable of being an actor, when required," he said, as Lord Brinsworth rose, reaching for the decanter so that he could pour another brandy for both himself and Frederick. "We need to decide what will be said and what we will pretend to arrange." He swallowed hard. "And what consequences there will be thereafter."

The Duke smiled sympathetically.

"No doubt you are concerned for Lady Georgina's welfare thereafter, should it become apparent that her father is a traitor," he said, with Frederick shrugging as though he cared very little, although he was quite certain it was in a less than convincing manner. "But there will be caution and care taken."

"Besides which," Lord Brinsworth added, his brow lifting, "you could always marry her yourself if she means that much to you." Seeing Frederick's sharp expression, he held up one hand, palm forward to ask Stratham to allow him to express his thought. "It would mean that she would keep her place in society, although there would still be the shame of her father's doings which would linger, I fear."

Frederick said nothing, grunting once and then turning his head away from Lord Brinsworth, as though this would dismiss the idea entirely. But, as the Duke and Lord Brinsworth began to discuss certain particulars with regard to Lord Kingham, Frederick found himself considering what Lord Brinsworth had suggested. After all, it was not as though the idea was a bad one. It was a rather wise suggestion for, if Frederick brought about a difficult situation for Lady Georgina by doing his duty, then might he not then go on to make it a little better by offering her his hand? It could very well be that she would not accept him, but Frederick quietly determined that, should it be required of him, he would offer. The thought of having Lady Georgina as his bride was an attractive prospect and Frederick could not help but warm to it. But, just as he thought of it, the memory of how she had appeared to him when he had told her the truth about their acquaintance came into his mind and his heart dropped like a stone.

He was quite sure that, after that, even if he were to ask, Lady Georgina would never accept him.

～

"LADY GEORGINA."

The lady did not stop walking.

"Lord Stratham," she said curtly, her eyes held fast away from his. "Good afternoon. Do excuse me, I have–"

"Would you not give me even a moment?" He fell into step beside her as she continued her promenade through the park, looking at her earnestly. "Lady Georgina, you must understand–"

"It is considered rude for a gentleman not to consider a young lady's wishes," she interrupted, her expression pinched as she kept her head turned a little away from him. "Lord Stratham, you can see that I am out walking with my mother and my friends, please allow me to enjoy their company without further interruption."

Frederick lifted one eyebrow, allowing his gaze to rest on the others who walked ahead. As far as he could see, Lady Matilda was walking with her beau, whilst Lady Kingham and Lady Kellingston walked together, their heads close as they spoke at length. Lady Georgina had been walking alone behind the rest and it was solely because of her position that Frederick had decided to come to speak with her.

"You have not forgiven me, then," he said, stiffly, as Lady Georgina remained pale-faced and now, tight-lipped. "You have not thought on what I have said."

Lady Georgina sniffed but said nothing and Frederick's jaw tightened as he tried his best to work out what he might say next. This was not what he had wanted. This was not the resolution he had hoped for, but what a foolish endeavor it had been to tell her the truth and somehow believe that all would be well! Of course she was injured, of course she was hurt by his lack of honesty towards her, but Frederick had hoped that Lady Georgina would understand *why* he had been forced to do such a thing.

"I had not ever expected to feel such emotion towards you, Lady Georgina," he said quietly, choosing to speak with an honesty and a forthrightness that did not often come to his lips. It felt strange to be in such a state, to have such a determination to tell her everything he thought, but Frederick welcomed the feeling, choosing not to allow it to overwhelm him and force him back into silence. "When we were first acquainted, I will admit that I sought you for my own reasons, due to the responsibilities which I have taken on. However, as time has gone on, I have found myself all the more eager for your company.

I have begun to look forward to the social events I have been invited to in the hope and sometimes in the knowledge that you will be there. Indeed, I have been berated by Lord Brinsworth for ever allowing myself to become so entangled with another!" This remark caused Lady Georgina to look at him sharply as if to state that she did not believe him, but Frederick nodded fervently, wanting to convince her that it was so. "If I could have told you the truth from the beginning, then I would have done so," he stated, unequivocally. "But I could not. Pray tell me you understand why I could not, my dear Lady Georgina."

She sighed, her gaze dropping away from his again.

"I will not state that I do not understand, Lord Stratham," she said, softly, "but rather that I am upset upon realizing that the person you now consider to be responsible for all of the terrible things that you have described must be someone close to me, else you would not have pursued my acquaintance." Her eyes searched his. "It must be my father."

Frederick held her gaze and did not hide the truth from her.

"He is someone we are considering, yes," he said, softly. "The intelligence we have received states that a gentleman whose title begins with a particular letter is the one who has been aiding the French and attempting to encourage and support the impending invasion. It would be wrong of us *not* to consider your father since he knows of my time in the army – a thing which you informed me about – and because his title fits that which we are looking at. We have investigated others whose titles also begin so, but none have proven correct. Your father remains the most likely..."

Lady Georgina's shoulders dropped.

"I know. I understand," she said, heavily. "But you must understand why I feel as I do."

"I do not understand fully, but I am attempting to do so," Frederick said, honestly. "Please believe me when I say that I have come to care for you in a manner which I never expected to and that this has caused me a good deal more difficulty than I had ever imagined!" A tiny smile crept across his lips. "It may be that your father is not at all involved and that we are quite wrong in this. But it would not have been right for myself, nor for the Duke or Lord Brinsworth, to do nothing at all. Our duty to King and country demands that we check every possibility."

Lady Georgina sighed heavily and dropped her head.

"I am aware of that," she stated, her voice firm but quiet. "But you truly cannot think it is my father, Lord Stratham! He is a gentleman of the *ton*, a man who has always done as society expects. He would not risk his reputation – nor that of his son – to aid the enemy! What would his purpose be in that? What would he gain?"

Frederick had to admit that Lady Georgina had asked some excellent questions, for he could not easily give her an answer.

"I do not know," he replied, truthfully. "However, I will say that I have seen many a gentleman do untoward and, quite frankly, treasonous, things without any hesitation and solely due to their own convictions."

"But not my father," Lady Georgina replied, with a sudden lift of her chin, fire blazing in her eyes. "I will agree with you, Lord Stratham, that there is much you must do. I will also agree that you have every right and reason to make certain that my father is *not* the man you are seeking, but I will tell you now that, when you complete your reconnaissance, you will discover that he quite innocent of all you believe him guilty of."

Spreading his hands, Frederick held Lady Georgina's gaze.

"And I shall be very glad of it," he said, honestly. "I know that it is exceedingly difficult to know the truth of the situation and all that is taking place, but I did want you to know. I wanted to be able to tell you the truth so that you would not be under any illusions. I would not have lies between us."

She looked back at him steadily and, for the first time since their meeting, there was a gentleness in her expression which encouraged Frederick somewhat. He did not say anything further and, for some moments, they simply held each other's gaze.

Lady Georgina let out a long breath.

"I am grateful for your honesty, Lord Stratham," she admitted, each word pulled from her as though she were, in fact, very unwilling to say such a thing. "I have thought on everything you have said." A twinkle appeared in her eyes for just a moment. "On *everything*, Lord Stratham."

Heat began to pour into Frederick's cheeks, but he did not look away from her, knowing precisely to what Lady Georgina was referring.

"I am glad I was able to speak so," he stated, unequivocally. "As I have said, Lady Georgina, I wanted you to know the truth in its entirety. I have no regrets in speaking so."

Her smile grew all the more.

"Give me some time to consider my response, Lord Stratham," she said, softly. "There *will* be one, I assure you, but at present, I have much to think on." Her smile dimmed just a little. "You will have a plan, I assume, as to how to discover the truth about my father."

Frederick nodded.

"We do."

She tilted her head, her eyes searching his face.

"And can I know of it?"

Hesitating, Frederick began to shake his head, only to stop and consider her carefully.

"I must be able to trust that you will not say a word to your father on this matter," he answered, slowly, seeing the slight frown which marred her brow. "If I cannot, then there is nothing that I could say to you at present."

He left the choice entirely in her hands, waiting for her to respond. It took some minutes but, eventually, Lady Georgina sighed, dropped her gaze, and shook her head.

"No, do not tell me," she said, heavily. "Just to make certain that I have not even a single temptation to say anything to him to make certain of his innocence." She gave him a small, sad smile. "But do speak to me thereafter about what has taken place, when you know for certain that my father has done nothing wrong."

Frederick nodded, his expression grave.

"Yes, of course, Lady Georgina," he promised, praying silently that her confidence in her father would not be misplaced. "I will do so just as soon as I can. You have my word."

CHAPTER ELEVEN

*I*t had taken every single modicum of Georgina's resolve not to ask what he had planned as regarded her father. Her heart had been crying out to her to ask, to discover the truth, and yet she had forced herself to remain silent, demanded that her lips did not ask a single question. She had been relieved that Lord Stratham had been willing to tell her what she had wanted to know, but also a little irritated that he had left the decision up to her. She had wanted him to tell her outright, without hesitation, so that she would not have to do anything other than listen, but when he had asked her to decide whether or not she should be told, Georgina had been forced to think more cautiously.

Still, even though she was convinced that she had done the right thing, it irritated her beyond belief that she was without any awareness of what Lord Stratham, Lord Brinsworth, and the Duke of Abernyte had planned. She wanted desperately to know it all but, at the same time, was glad that she did not. Georgina was quite certain that her father would not be found to bear any guilt in any matter related to the French and was looking forward to a time when that could be proven entirely.

But who would that leave?

Her mind began to run through all of the gentlemen she knew who bore a title with the letter 'K'. No doubt, the Duke and Lord Stratham had made certain that all of those in London who had such a title had already been checked by either one or both of them, but that did not mean that there could not be someone else other than her father left! Perhaps the person responsible had already left London and had gone to Bath or elsewhere.

Although that does not account for the man who threw me from my carriage.

Grimacing, Georgina rose from her seat in the drawing-room, the book she had been attempting to read now lying idly on the side of the chair. Wandering to the window, she looked through the lace curtain onto the street below.

The men that Lord Stratham had promised would protect her were still very much present, although she did not know who, in particular, they were. Men were standing, conversing, laughing, and walking up and down the busy square and the park and Georgina knew that, amongst them, there were her protectors. There was no reason for Lord Stratham to remove them from the townhouse and therefore, Georgina found herself quite at peace.

"Georgina?"

She turned, a little surprised to see none other than Lady Matilda entering the room.

"Matilda!" she exclaimed, glancing at the clock which ticked away gently on the mantelpiece. "Whatever are you doing here? Afternoon calls are not until...." She trailed off, seeing the sadness in her friend's expression and immediately hurrying over to her. Grasping her hand, Georgina looked into Lady Matilda's eyes, growing more and more concerned with very moment that passed.

"Whatever is the matter?" she asked, as Lady Matilda shook her head, her lips quivering. "Has something happened with Lord Bulford?"

Lady Matilda shook her head and a wave of relief washed over Georgina. She had feared that the courtship had come to an end, and that was the reason for Lady Matilda's sorrow but that, it seemed, was still intact.

"Mother wants us to leave London."

Georgina stared at Lady Matilda in shock.

"Whatever do you mean?" she exclaimed, as Lady Matilda dropped her head, blinking back tears. "You are being courted by Lord Bulford! Why would your mother wish to take you from that?"

"I do not know!" Lady Matilda wailed, pulling her hands from Georgina's, making her way across the room so that she might throw herself into a chair. Leaning forward, she put her head in her hands, her voice thin and punctuated by sobs as she continued to speak. "She came to tell me only this morning that she is thinking about leaving London, and that I should begin to prepare myself for our departure!" Tears began streaming down her face. "I do not understand it! I have come to care for Lord Bulford and, indeed, I am quite certain that he cares for me also, for he has been speaking of the future and what may be and...."

She could not speak any longer, her voice breaking completely as she gave in to sobs.

Georgina was there in a moment, one hand wrapping around her friend's shoulders as she struggled to think of what to say. It did not make any sense for Lady Kellingston to leave London now, not in the middle of the Season, and certainly not when her daughter had such an excellent prospect! She would be ruining Lady Matilda's future and, quite possibly, making it so that Lady Matilda would never find herself with the chance to wed again. No doubt the *ton* would think that there was some sort of scandal involved in her being rushed away from London so soon, and the rumors which followed could damage Lady Matilda severely.

"She did not say a word as to *why* you had to leave?" Georgina asked, gently, as Lady Matilda shook her head, her ringlets flying. "There must surely be a reason. Mayhap she is doing all she can to make certain that you are kept quite safe, Matilda."

"I do not want to leave!" Lady Matilda wailed, her eyes still flooded with tears. "Not when I have so much to stay for! In a few weeks – even in a few days – I could find myself betrothed!"

"Then you *must* stay," Georgina replied, firmly, feeling deep sympathy for her friend. "I will insist on it. If your mother must return to the estate for whatever reason, then *you* can stay here with us."

Lady Matilda's sorrowful eyes lifted to hers, her cheeks damp with tears and her lips trembling.

"Do... do you think your mother would agree?" she asked a tiny flicker of hope now in her expression. "Truly?"

"I am quite certain that she would!" Georgina replied with alacrity. In fact, why do we not go to ask her this very moment!"

She rose to her feet, but Lady Matilda shook her head.

"My mother is speaking with yours," she explained, as Georgina sank back into her chair, a frown growing. "No doubt she will explain what is happening and her reasons for making that choice, even though *I* am not permitted to know of it!"

She grimaced and sat back in the chair, her eyes closing as though she was left with nothing but weariness over what had occurred.

"Nevertheless," Georgina determined, rising from her chair once more and going towards the door, "I will go and suggest that you stay here with us for the time being." She spoke with a confidence that she did not truly feel, for there was a very good chance that her mother would refuse, in which case, there was nothing more that could be done for Lady Matilda. "Rest here. And ring the bell," she suggested with a smile. "Order tea and cakes for yourself. I am certain that you will feel better after that."

Lady Matilda's chin wobbled and for a moment, Georgina feared that she would once again burst into tears but, much to her relief, Lady Matilda merely nodded and smiled. With a small sigh of relief, Georgina stepped out of the door and made her way to the large parlor, where she expected to find both her mother and Lady Kellingston.

Her assumption was correct. She could hear Lady Kellingston's voice, high and frantic, floating through the hallway towards her and, as she drew nearer, Georgina's concern began to grow.

"It is simply because I *must*," she heard Lady Kellingston say. "The Season has nothing for her now. Lord Bulford is not a suitable gentleman, I am quite sure of it!"

"Whatever is wrong with him?" Georgina shared her mother's exclaimed surprise. "He is genteel, with a good title and an excellent fortune. His character appears to be quite kind also, does it not? He clearly is interested in Lady Matilda, and I am certain that, should he continue to court her, then he would soon consider marriage."

"No!" came the cried exclamation from Lady

Kellingston. "I cannot have it. I am certain that he means her ill."

Georgina chose that moment to step into the room, clearing her throat gently as she did so. She had to pretend that she had heard nothing of their discussion thus far, although her heart was beating with a little more concern, given all that she had overheard.

"Good morning, Lady Kellingston," she said, closing the door softly behind her. "I am sorry to hear that you are thinking of leaving London. I can understand Lady Matilda's sorrow at such news. I had wondered, Mama," she directed her attention towards her mother, "whether or not Lady Matilda might reside here with us for a short while if Lady Kellingston is required back at their estate? After all, Lord Bulford is courting her, and I have heard that he is an excellent gentleman, and it is clear that he cares for Lady Matilda fervently. I am certain that there will be a proposal very soon, and I should very much like to share in that happiness when it comes."

She kept her voice light and her smile fixed, finding herself doubting that Lord Bulford was, in fact, the real reason for Lady Kellingston to suddenly have the desire to depart London. After all, if she had truly had such a grave concern over Lord Bulford, then surely she would not have allowed Lady Matilda to accept the gentleman's court! There was the slight possibility that Lord Bulford had only revealed his true character thereafter, but Georgina could not find a way to believe it. He was not known as a rake, nor a scoundrel, and there was certainly nothing untoward being spoken of him in society. Therefore, Georgina was quite convinced in her own mind that Lady Kellingston had another reason entirely for wishing to leave London at such a time, although she could not imagine what it could be.

"That is very kind of you, Lady Georgina, but I do not think it is possible." Lady Kellingston's voice shook, but she appeared, outwardly, rather composed. "Lady Matilda must be pulled from Lord Bulford's side just as soon as possible."

"Oh?" Georgina asked, throwing a glance at her mother, and noticing the way that her eyebrow arched, as if to suggest that she found everything Lady Kellingston said to be more than a little questionable. "I had not heard that Lord Bulford's character was in question." She came a little further into the room, an idea forming in her mind. "What is it about him which has provoked this reaction, might I ask?" Spreading her hands, she shook her head lightly in apparent dismay. "It is always very difficult when one does not know the truth about a gentleman."

"Indeed," Lady Kellingston replied, sounding very grave indeed, "but I do not think that it is required of me to say such things about him. I am sure, in time, you will discover the truth for yourself."

Again, Georgina looked to her mother and, this time, Lady Kingham caught her eye. There was a touch of color in her cheeks as if to suggest that she was displeased by Lady Kellingston's response, perhaps believing – as Georgina did – that there was no truth in what was being said.

"That might be a little too late, however," Lady Kingham replied, carefully. "For surely you would like to tell Georgina what the difficulty is, so that she might, in turn, tell her friends, so that they may know why they must avoid Lord Bulford at all costs!" She tilted her head enquiringly. "After all, you would not want Georgina or any of her acquaintances to find themselves in the very same position as Lady Matilda, would you?"

"Precisely," Georgina agreed hurriedly, wanting to

make certain that Lady Kellingston could not easily slip away without giving her the required answers. "I am sure there are many more young ladies who would immediately hope to consider Lord Bulford, should they be given an opportunity. If it is known that Lady Matilda is gone from London and that he is free once more, then he will soon be quite surrounded!" She closed her eyes tightly, screwing up her features as if in horror at the very thought. "I must know what I can say to make certain that the truth is known of him."

This seemed to bring Lady Kellingston a great deal of difficulty, for whilst she did not answer, she seemed to attempt to do so, opening her mouth and then closing it again a moment later. This occurred a few times until she eventually put her hands over her face and let out a shriek of either exasperation or upset. Georgina's eyes flared wide with shock, as she stared at Lady Kellingston, only for her mother to flap her hands at Georgina hurriedly, before going to her friend. Quickly, Georgina left the room and, despite her desire to linger by the door and hear all that was going on, good manners and her responsibility to her friend Lady Matilda, forced her to return to the drawing-room.

Her heart was pounding with the shock of what she had witnessed. Lady Kellingston seemed to have quite lost all composure for a moment, appearing to be overcome with emotion. Quite what was going on, Georgina could not say but certainly, Lady Kellingston was in a great deal of distress. Nothing made sense and Georgina was more than desperate to discern the truth, fearful now for what lay ahead for Lady Matilda.

"Well?"

Almost the moment that Georgina had opened the door,

Lady Matilda was by her side, her red-rimmed eyes staring fiercely at her.

"What did she say? Am I permitted to stay?"

"I – I do not know, Matilda," Georgina replied, as gently as she could, settling one hand on Lady Matilda's shoulder. "Your mother is most grievously upset, and my mother is attempting to discover why she is in such a state. However," she continued, seeing Lady Matilda's eyes flare wide, "I have asked that you be permitted to stay here with us. Your mother has refused but it may be that, once my mother speaks to her, she might have a change of heart."

Lady Matilda pressed her lips together hard, her eyes suddenly filled with a fire which Georgina had not expected to see. Neither did she burst into the flood of tears that Georgina had been anticipating. Instead, she simply lifted her chin, turned on her heel, and marched across to the window.

"I will elope," she said firmly, as Georgina stared after her, now dumbstruck with shock. "If Lord Bulford cares for me as he has said, then my mother's actions will not prevent my happiness. I will write to him at once and find a way to inform him of all that has taken place."

Georgina swallowed hard, trying to find something to say, but finding that her throat was dry, her tongue sticking to the roof of her mouth. To elope was a serious matter, and a lot of gossip could come from such an act thereafter. After all, if a gentleman and a lady ran away to Scotland to marry, then the *ton* would, no doubt, wonder why they had cause to do such a thing – and would speak of their ideas as though they were facts. There would be whispers of scandal, whispers of impropriety and those whispers would very easily stick to both Lady Matilda and her husband for some time. She dropped into a chair, suddenly feeling completely discomposed by the events of the day. Had Matilda truly just suggested...?

"Elope...?"

"You think it a foolish idea, but you have not felt as I do at present," Lady Matilda stated, with a somewhat dramatic air. "You do not know what it is like to have such depth of feeling for one particular gentleman."

Georgina hesitated before she responded, finding that she wanted very much to state that yes, she knew precisely what Lady Matilda spoke of but, as she began to answer, she stopped herself and forced herself not to mention him. It was extraordinary how much she wanted to state his name, how she wanted to tell Lady Matilda that the feelings she spoke of were akin to those within her own heart, for Lord Stratham, for Georgina had not, until now, truly considered all that she felt for the gentleman. She had felt all manner of things, from frustration, to upset, to a deep sense of solidarity which had slowly grown into something more. Something she now recognized.

"You are choosing to remain silent on this matter," Lady Matilda said softly, as Georgina caught her eye, having been too lost in her own thoughts to realize just how keenly her friend had been watching her. "I will not ask why. But I must beg of you to remain silent about all that I have told you, Georgina."

Georgina's shoulders slumped.

"You cannot think that I would go to your mother and tell her all that you have said, surely?" she replied, a little hurt that her friend would think so little of her. "There is a friendship and a trust between us that I would never think of breaking."

Lady Matilda smiled, her eyes clear now that she had a plan in her mind and a resolution as regarded Lord Bulford.

"It is not that I do not trust you, nor that I think so little of your friendship that I ask such a thing, my dear Georgina," she explained, "but only that, out of your great concern for me, you might think it best to tell my mother what I have planned." She shrugged. "An attempt to protect me, I suppose."

"I would not do so," Georgina promised. "I confess that I am confused as to why your mother thinks so little of Lord Bulford and, indeed, can see nothing of an issue with his character nor his status." She leaned forward in her seat, her hands clasping tightly as her elbows rested on her knees. "I pray that you make a wise decision, however," she finished, praying silently that she too was making the right choice in choosing to remain quiet about her friend's intentions. "And most of all, my dear Matilda, I wish you happy."

CHAPTER TWELVE

"My Lord."

Frederick looked up in frustration. He was just finishing final preparations for this evening's meeting and had not expected to be disturbed.

"What is it?" he asked, gruffly, as his butler stepped into the room, looking, Frederick noted, a little unsure of himself.

"Forgive me, my Lord," the butler said, bowing slightly. "But there is a slight... issue as regards a particular visitor."

Frederick's heart lurched. Had Lord Kingham realized that this was nothing more than a ruse? Had he sent someone to tell Frederick that he would *not* be attending this evening, to prove to him that he would not be so easily caught?

"What is it?" he asked, turning a little more towards the butler. "Is it the Duke of Abernyte?"

The butler shook his head, his hands clasping tightly together in front of him as though in an attempt to give him the courage to tell Frederick exactly what was occurring.

"My Lord, there is a young lady to see you," he said,

sending a chill straight through Frederick as he stared at him in astonishment. "I could not very well send her away, but I do not know what else I ought to do. She is quite insistent." He glanced into Frederick's eyes and then looked away as a flush of heat poured into Frederick's cheeks. No doubt the butler – and the rest of his staff – would now think that there was something untoward going on, or that he was having some sort of secret liaison with a young lady of note. Perhaps they thought her already wed and he playing her husband false! Closing his eyes tightly for a moment, Frederick cleared his throat gruffly.

"What is the name of this young lady?" he asked, his words clipped. "Did she give as reason as to why she has called?"

The butler did not lift his gaze to Frederick's.

"It is Lady Georgina Fielding, I believe," he said quietly. "She did not give her name but one of our maids recognized the maid who attended with her."

It took all of Frederick's strength not to exclaim aloud. Lady Georgina? What was she doing here? And at such a late hour?

"She will not depart, my Lord, not without seeing you," the butler added, as Frederick stared at him unblinkingly, horrified at this news. "And I could not simply force her from the house. She is waiting in the drawing-room."

Gathering himself, Frederick sighed, ran one hand over his eyes and nodded.

"Of course you could not," he stated, tightly. "Very well, I will go to speak to her." He lifted one eyebrow towards the butler. "You say that she has a maid with her?"

"Her lady's maid, yes," the butler answered, as Frederick nodded.

"Then send another to the drawing-room," Frederick

stated firmly, hoping that this would, in some way, alleviate some of the impropriety of their meeting. "I would not have the lady's reputation damaged in any way so, if any of my staff think that they will share with their friends and acquaintances that Lady Georgina was present here at this late hour, then you know what will happen. Please ensure their discretion." The butler nodded at once, his head lifting just a little as though to state that he was quite certain that the staff – *his* staff – would not be inclined towards gossip. Or, if they were, that he would make quite certain that they did *not* do so! "Then I will be down momentarily," Frederick finished, turning back towards his desk. "Thank you."

Frederick waited until the butler had left the room and the door clicked shut behind him, before closing his eyes and letting out a long breath. Pressing both hands down on the table, he let his head drop forward. Whatever was Lady Georgina doing here? Yes, she had been present two nights ago when he had – supposedly accidentally – let slip about a meeting which was to take place with a stoolpigeon who knew those within the *ton* who might be involved with the French, but he had never thought that she would then determine to come to join him at the very hour the meeting was supposedly to take place!

"Lord Stratham." Astonished, Frederick spun around, only to see Lady Georgina framed in the doorway, her eyes fixed on his. She was not smiling, but her expression was quite severe, with a firmness about her mouth and steel in her eyes. "I could not simply wait in the drawing-room for fear that you would leave without me," she said calmly, coming into the room. "My mother is abed with a headache and believes that I have retired early. Therefore, I had no difficulty in slipping away." One shoulder lifted. "My father has already gone out to play cards, although I am certain that you believe he is doing something else entirely."

There was something quite wonderful about her at that moment and, whilst Frederick wanted very much to demand that she leave the house and return home, he found that he could not. The boldness and courage which she had expressed in doing as she had done made him think so highly of her that he could not find the right words to speak. She was magnificent, he considered, seeing the determination in her eyes and finding himself rather overwhelmed by her. There was, of course, the matter of propriety and the fact that her reputation could be quite ruined if this situation were ever discovered by another member of the *ton*, but it seemed that Lady Georgina considered that a risk worth taking.

Besides which, I would have no concern whatsoever, should it be required of me to marry her.

A little embarrassed by his own thoughts, Frederick cleared his throat and took a small step towards her.

"Lady Georgina," he said, spreading his hands. "Whatever are you doing here?"

She lifted her chin.

"If you are going to attempt to capture my father, then I should like to be present," she stated, her eyes narrowing slightly. "I do not believe that he is in any way guilty but, given that you are quite certain that he *is* so, then I want to be there when the meeting takes place." Her cheeks colored. "I am not as unobservant as you might think me, Lord Stratham," she continued, a little more loudly. "I was all too aware of what you suggested to my father two nights ago. I know that this supposed meeting with the stoolpigeon is precisely the trap you want him to fall into."

"You were not even present by me when I spoke," Frederick replied, but Lady Georgina waved a hand.

"I was close enough," she retorted, as though she was upset that he thought so little of her. "I knew that you had every intention of speaking to my father, so I made certain that I was always nearby whenever you were close to him." She smiled mirthlessly. "I am still quite convinced that my father has no guilt whatsoever, but I am going to be present to make quite certain of it."

Frederick wanted to argue, wanted to state quite clearly that she was *not* coming and that, therefore, she would have no other choice but to return home, but a quiet voice within him told him that it was foolishness to even try. Sighing heavily, he ran one hand over his eyes.

"You risk a great deal, Lady Georgina," he murmured, as her expression softened as she realized that he intended to permit her to join him. "What if you are seen?"

"Then I shall accept the consequences without hesitation," she replied, coming a little nearer to him and looking up into his face. "In the hope that, at the end of it all, he might be saved from the greatest shame."

Knowing precisely what she referred to, Frederick caught his breath as the urge to lean down and kiss her full on the lips swamped him. It took him a moment to thrust that away, and he was forced to turn aside from her so that he would not do as he so eagerly wished.

"Then we must depart," he stated, looking back at her. "I do hope, Lady Georgina, that you know exactly what may face you." A frown pulled at his brow. "What if your father *does* appear? What then?"

Lady Georgina's expression did not change.

"Then I shall know that everything I thought of him was quite wrong," she replied, coming towards the door and walking past him through it. "And I shall be able to return to my mother and tell her all, having been witness and party to it." Her voice echoed gently as they made their way into the corridor. "But I do not believe for a moment that you will find him there, Lord Stratham." She threw a glance back towards him and he was surprised at the deep concern in her eyes. "In fact, I believe that I *may* know the true culprit, Lord Stratham. And it is certainly not my father."

~

FREDERICK HAD NOT ASKED Lady Georgina anything more as they traveled to the meeting place. He had not wanted to do so in front of the two maids who were with them – both of whom were wide-eyed and white-faced – and in addition, because he did not believe that Lady Georgina would tell him the truth, even if he asked her for it. To have such a firm belief that her father was *not* the man they required, as well as being quite certain that she knew who else was at fault, was certainly of great interest, but there was a part of Frederick that believed she was saying such things only in the hope that her father would be proven innocent. Quite what she would do or how she would react when he appeared, as Frederick believed he would, he could not say. Would she hold it against Frederick personally? Would what he hoped for – nay, prayed for – be gone from his future entirely?

"We are here." The supposed meeting place was down by the docks and even now, Frederick could smell the salt on the air. He gave her one long look, her face half-hidden as the dim lantern light from within the carriage cast great shadows across them both. "Are you quite certain you wish to join us, Lady Georgina? I could have you wait in the carriage and–"

"*Quite* certain." She did not wait for him but, the very moment the door opened, made to step outside. Frederick drew in a deep breath and stepped out also, turning his head this way and that as his coachman stood by the horses, keeping them as quiet as he could.

"There."

A bobbing light in the distance caught his attention and, after offering Lady Georgina his arm, the two of them set off together. They did not have to walk for too long, for the Duke of Abernyte and Lord Brinsworth soon appeared, hurrying towards them. They stopped in surprise as they took in Lady Georgina's presence, but Frederick merely shook his head and shrugged, silently telling them both that he could not have prevented her from attending.

"Good evening, Lord Stratham... Lady Georgina." The Duke bowed and cast another curious glance towards Frederick. "You have decided to join us, I see."

"I would not be prevented," Lady Georgina replied, crisply. "Now, where are we to wait?"

Frederick shook his head to himself but caught the Duke's grin in the moonlight. Evidently, he thought well of Lady Georgina's determination, even though Frederick was still quite uncertain about her presence.

"This way," Lord Brinsworth muttered, his tone suggesting that he was deeply unhappy with the lady's arrival. "I do hope that you are prepared, Lady Georgina. What will follow will not be pleasant."

Lady Georgina lifted her head and met Lord Brinsworth's eyes and, even in the gloom, Frederick felt the intensity of it.

"I do not think that there will be *any* unpleasantness, Lord Brinsworth," she retorted, sharply. "Pray, lead on."

Despite his uncertainty and his worry, Frederick could not help but grin at the lady's tenacity. She stalked off ahead of him as the Duke led the way and, as Frederick fell into step behind her, he found himself praying that all that she believed, all that she hoped, would prove to be right.

"It has been two hours now."

There was something in the way that Lady Georgina lifted her head at this remark that told Frederick that she had been fully expecting it to be so.

"Then he is not coming."

"Or," Lady Georgina interrupted, her voice a little tight, "my father is *not* the one you seek."

Frederick let out a long, slow breath. He could not quite believe that it had been two hours, for it had seemed to be far longer than that! Shifting slowly, he rose from his seat atop a wooden barrel and stretched. His heart was being pulled in two directions for, whilst he was extremely glad indeed that Lady Georgina was to be spared the heartache of seeing her father being pulled out as the one from the *ton* who had been aiding the French, he was also deeply frustrated that their plans had come to naught.

"Then someone must have told him," Lord Brinsworth muttered darkly. Frederick had no doubt as to who he meant and, given the exclamation which came from the lady, Lady Georgina understood it also.

"I have not said a single word!" she retorted, her words ice. "It may surprise you, but there is a possibility that you are wrong in this matter." She drew in a long breath, turning her head towards Frederick. "In fact, I believe that I might know who it is that you must consider." She fell silent for some moments until, eventually, Frederick took a small step closer to her. His hand found hers in the darkness and he pressed it gently, wondering who it was that she had in mind and wondering silently if she was finding it difficult to speak their name due to their closeness. Lady Georgina pressed his hand in return. She took in a long breath and then set her shoulders. "I believe," she said, "that it may be Lady Kellingston."

Frederick allowed this news to pass through his mind for a few moments before he spoke. There was an air of anticipation growing between them all, heightened a little by the darkness. The Duke of Abernyte had not said a word, and neither had Lord Brinsworth. There was nothing but silence.

"Lady Kellingston." Lord Brinsworth's tone was one of disbelief. "Lady Georgina, with all due respect to you for your consideration and the like, we are seeking a *gentleman*." He cleared his throat as Frederick pressed Lady Georgina's hand tightly, not wanting her to react to Lord Brinsworth's tone. "Lady Kellingston is not who we are searching for."

"I believe it is." Lady Georgina's voice rang out in the darkness, firm and clear. "You may have made a mistake when it comes to the specific title, but I believe that it *is* Lady Kellingston who has been aiding the enemy."

"And for what reason?" Frederick asked, speaking in a much gentler manner than his companion. "She is a lady of the *ton* who is seeking to present her daughter to society in the hope of a good match. Why should she have any eagerness to help the French?"

The clouds parted just as Lady Georgina turned to him,

her eyes meeting his as her features became bathed in moonlight.

"Because," she began, quietly, "Lady Kellingston's son, the current Lord Kellingston himself, has been captured by the French."

Her words hit Frederick full in the face, leaving him stunned.

"She is desperate for his return and, as I understand it, his uncle has been doing what he can, but there has been no progress whatsoever," she continued, speaking quickly so that the words tumbled out one after the other. "She has no other avenue left. Therefore, given that she wants nothing more than her son's return, she has offered to aid the enemy in return for keeping her son safe." She lifted one shoulder. "Mayhap they have promised that, in time, they will return him."

Frederick nodded slowly, his hand still holding hers whilst he rubbed at his chin with the other, thoughtfully. It did make sense and it might very well have been that the title of 'Lord K' that they had been given had been nothing more than a mistake. After all, it would not be usual for a lady to be involved in such matters and, therefore, it would almost be assumed that it was a gentleman. He had not known about Lord Kellingston and certainly had never even thought to consider his mother. But it seemed that Lady Georgina was, in fact, a little wiser about such matters than they.

The Duke of Abernyte cleared his throat.

"I had heard that Lord Kellingston was at war," he said, slowly, coming to stand a little nearer to them all. "But I had not realized that he had been captured."

Lady Georgina nodded.

"I am certain it is so," she stated, although Frederick

heard a slight wobble in her voice which spoke of upset and
sorrow. "Lady Matilda is my dear friend, and we speak
often of her brother." Her shoulders slumped. "She, and
equally her mother, is frustrated that nothing appears to
have been done about securing his release as yet, and from
what she said the last time that we spoke of the affair, it
seems that her mother is becoming quite desperate."

"And thus has gone to the French," the Duke
murmured, nodding slowly. "Might I ask, Lady Georgina, if
there are any other reasons for your belief of Lady
Kellingston's guilt in this matter? Anything which she has
said or done?"

Again, there came a short pause but, eventually, she
spoke. Frederick felt her tremble slightly as she did so and
felt his heart swell with sympathy for her. This must be
exceedingly difficult indeed, given that it was her friend's
mother whom she was speaking of. Again, he considered
that Lady Georgina showed both great courage and determination and for that, he was very grateful indeed.

"Lady Kellingston intends to leave London," she said, as
Lord Brinsworth came a little closer, listening intently to all
that was said. "She came to see my mother yesterday
evening, in such a distressed state, declaring that it is for
Lady Matilda's sake that they depart."

"Lady Matilda?" Frederick repeated, frowning. "But
she is being courted by Lord Bulford. Why should Lady
Kellingston wish to separate them?"

Lady Georgina shook her head.

"She states that she has discovered something about
Lord Bulford which does not please her and that she is,
therefore, protecting Lady Matilda by doing this, but I do
not believe it." Her tone changed and Frederick could
almost taste the slight bitterness that now lined her words.

"She is using Lord Bulford as an excuse, but there is nothing the matter with the gentleman. Lady Matilda is quite heartbroken and, indeed, I believe they intend to elope." She shut her eyes for a moment and Frederick could not help but release her hand to slip his arm around her waist. "I think it would perhaps be best if they did so, *before* the truth about Lady Kellingston comes to light."

Frederick let out a long breath, blowing it out slowly as he took in everything Lady Georgina had said.

"Then she must have overheard what I spoke of to your father," he said, realizing that not only had Lady Kellingston been present two nights ago, but also nearby when he had spoken of this supposed meeting. "She has taken fright, believing what I said to Lord Kingham to be quite true."

Lord Brinsworth nodded.

"She thinks that we *are* meeting with a stoolpigeon who will tell us of all those involved in the affairs with the French," he said, as Frederick nodded. "Therefore, she is leaving London for fear of being discovered. Once back at her son's estate, she might make plans to relocate elsewhere, somewhere that she cannot be discovered unless by design."

"She is to leave by the end of the week," Lady Georgina interrupted, "but I am sure that Lady Matilda will elope before then. Please—" She paused for a moment, trying to catch her breath before she continued, clearly finding the matter very distressing indeed. "Please, do not speak to her before that has occurred. Lady Matilda must be able to wed without delay, else she will have no happiness for the rest of her days."

Frederick pulled her close despite the fact that there were two other gentlemen present.

"We will take every precaution," he promised, quietly.

"Speak to Lady Matilda. Let us know what she says and, thereafter, we will arrange to speak with Lady Kellingston. She must be unaware of our intentions, however, until it is much too late."

Lady Georgina leaned against his shoulder and, despite himself, Frederick rested his cheek against the top of her head for a few moments.

"Thank you, Lord Stratham," he heard her mumble, realizing now just how weary and distressed she was. "Thank you, for Lady Matilda's sake."

"We will be careful and cautious," the Duke confirmed, as Lady Georgina remained precisely where she was, close to Frederick. "Thank you, Lady Georgina, this has been... enlightening."

"Thank you," Lord Brinsworth murmured, clearly now a little embarrassed and regretful over how sharply he had spoken to her previously. "Forgive me for my lack of consideration, Lady Georgina. As you can imagine, this has been a difficult time, but that is no excuse for how I reacted."

Lady Georgina lifted her head. "Thank you, Lord Brinsworth," she replied calmly, despite, Frederick was certain, the tumult which must, at present, be going on within her heart and mind. "I only hope that this is the end of the matter. And I pray that Lady Matilda will find her happiness before it is too late. She deserves that, at the very least."

"I will make certain it is so," Frederick stated, firmly. "I shall speak to Lord Bulford myself and make quite certain that he has the fastest of horses available to him."

"He can use my carriage if he so wishes also," the Duke put in, making Frederick smile ruefully.

It was not out of care and consideration for the lady that he offered such a thing, but rather that, in doing so, he would make certain that the elopement took place in the shortest possible time.

"That is very kind of you all," Lady Georgina answered, quietly. "Lord Stratham, might you return me home now?" She looked up into his face and even in the moonlight, Frederick could see the strain in her features. "I am tired."

"But of course." The urge to wrap his arm around her once more was too strong for him to turn from and he did so at once, pulling her close so that he might comfort her more than anything else. "At once, Lady Georgina."

She leaned into him as they walked away from their meeting spot, her steps slow and her head drooping with fatigue as they made their way to Frederick's waiting carriage. Not a word was spoken between them until they were both at the carriage, the silence seeming to be an additional comfort in itself.

"You have been so very kind, Lord Stratham," Lady Georgina murmured, as she settled into her seat. "To have permitted me to join you, to have allowed me to sit with you all as you waited… I am very grateful."

Frederick smiled wryly.

"I hardly think I had the choice, Lady Georgina," he answered, making to take his seat, only for her to beckon him to sit beside her rather than opposite. "But I do find your courage and your willingness to speak when it involves a friend to be worthy of the greatest amount of admiration and respect." Sitting down, he half turned towards her, looking down into her eyes and seeing just how carefully she watched him. "I think you the most wonderful lady in all the world."

Lady Georgina said nothing in response. Instead, she gave him a tired yet beautiful smile, before leaning so that she might rest her head on his shoulder. Frederick closed his eyes as he leaned back against the squabs, finding himself both very contented and very weary indeed. With a great sigh, he reached up and rapped on the roof, with the carriage moving off in an instant. This evening's work was at an end, but the final unveiling was still to come.

The two maids were, perhaps fortunately, not witness to this, as they had both fallen asleep during the long wait, curled into the corners of the seats.

CHAPTER THIRTEEN

"*I* am quite prepared."

Georgina tried to smile but inwardly felt as though her heart were slowly being pulled apart. "He will be here very soon, I am sure," she said softly, glancing out of the window as they waited together for the arrival of Lord Bulford. "I do hope that it all goes as it should, Matilda." Reaching for her friend's hand, she grasped it tightly. "I do care for you very much, you know."

Lady Matilda smiled back at Georgina, her eyes so bright that they almost dazzled her.

"We are very good friends, are we not?" she asked, as Georgina nodded. "You have done much to help me, Georgina. I shall not forget it."

Georgina swallowed hard, praying that God would keep Lady Matilda from ever knowing that it had been she who had realized the truth about Lady Kellingston.

"Thank you, Matilda," she replied, hearing the noise of conversation and laughter coming from the drawing-room just across the hall from them. They had been shown into Lord Brinsworth's small parlor where, he had murmured into Georgina's ear, they would have an excellent view of the street. Quite what Lord Stratham, Lord Brinsworth, and the Duke of Abernyte had done or said to Lord Bulford, Georgina did not know – but at the very least, she was aware that the elopement had been agreed upon and arranged with the greatest speed. Lord Bulford was to take the Duke's carriage and Lord Stratham had made certain that fresh horses – the very best – were waiting for them at the inns they would stop at. Georgina could see the excitement in Lady Matilda's eyes and, whilst she was very happy for her friend, she could not pretend that she did not feel sorrow and upset as well. After all, she could not say when she might next see Lady Matilda again, nor what the consequences would be that might follow thereafter. She had no idea what might happen to Lady Kellingston nor how it would affect Lady Matilda, but Georgina hoped that her friend would be spared the very worst.

Lady Matilda glanced behind her, a slight frown crossing her brow.

"I do hope that Mama will not come searching for me. It took much persuasion for her to attend Lord Brinsworth's soiree this evening and she did speak of leaving quite early so that we could make certain we were rested for tomorrow's travel."

"He is here!" Georgina spoke excitedly and heard Lady Matilda gasp as she turned back to the window, seeing the carriage which Georgina had spotted seconds before. "Come, you must go!"

Lady Matilda let out a small exclamation of delight, turned, and pulled Georgina into an embrace. Georgina returned it, hiding her tears as she said farewell to her friend.

"Do write to me the very first moment that you can,"

she begged, as Lady Matilda nodded, already pulling away. "Let me know that you are Lady Bulford!"

"I shall," Lady Matilda promised, hurrying to the door, and then stopping suddenly to turn her head back again towards Georgina. "And write to me when you are Lady Stratham."

Georgina did not have time to reply for, with a broad smile and a joyous expression on her face, Lady Matilda turned and made her way from the room. She let out a long breath and closed her eyes, reaching out to press one hand against the wall as the need to steady herself came over her. She did not hear the door open and close again, nor see Lord Stratham as he came towards her.

"She is gone, then."

Georgina shivered, opening her eyes, and then turning towards him.

"Yes," she said, knowing that there was great impropriety in being alone with Lord Stratham but finding that she did not care. "She is gone." She turned her gaze to the window and saw the carriage pull away with both Lord Bulford and Lady Matilda inside. Her heart ached terribly but she forced her head up, drawing in a deep breath. "Then it is time."

Lord Stratham's hand rested lightly on her back as he looked into her eyes.

"How do you fare?"

Swallowing hard, Georgina did not immediately answer.

"I am sorrowful," she answered, truthfully. "I am very glad that Lady Matilda has gone with Lord Bulford, even though I do not think that eloping is always a wise decision."

"But in this case, it has helped her immensely."

Georgina nodded, seeing the sympathy in his hazel eyes, and finding herself comforted.

"Precisely," she answered, recalling just how much she had drawn from him during their time together at the docks. He had not had much opportunity to forbid her from joining him, that much was certain, but he had given her the opportunity to speak as she thought, to express what she needed and, thereafter, had thanked her for it all. Had it not been for his willingness and his support, then Georgina might have found herself in a very different situation now.

"We should make our way to the dining room," Lord Stratham murmured, their gazes still locked as Georgina's heart began to quicken, lost in what she saw in his eyes. "There is more that I wish to say to you, Lady Georgina, but now is not the right moment to do so."

Her lips curved into a small, wry smile.

"Indeed, I feel myself to be in much the same position," she answered, finding herself eager to tell him the truth of what she felt, even though there was more required of them yet. "Perhaps in a few days?"

"I shall be glad to speak to you then," he promised, his smile tender. "Our hearts will, perhaps, be a little less burdened then."

She nodded, not trusting herself to speak as, turning, they made their way from the room, not spotted or noted by anyone. Georgina was relieved that her mother was a little less severe in her supervision this evening. That was in part thanks to the Duke of Abernyte, who had made certain that his mother was present this evening. As fate would have it, Lady Brinsworth – Lord Brinsworth's mother – was present that evening also and, unbeknownst to Georgina, knew her mother from years past. Therefore, their meeting had been one of great interest and mutual happiness, and much to Georgina's relief, Lady Kingham had been too overcome with delight at being in her company again to pay Georgina much attention. She could only hope that Lady Kingham would continue to be entirely unaware of Georgina's whereabouts – at least, for the next few minutes.

Her stomach tightened as she walked into the dining room with Lord Stratham by her side. His presence was a comfort, but she was still all too aware of what was to take place very soon.

"Are you quite certain that you wish to be here, Lady Georgina?" Lord Stratham's voice was soft, his eyes searching hers as she turned to glance at him. "You need not remain if you would prefer. It is not required of you."

Georgina straightened her shoulders, her chin lifting as the same, familiar determination came back into her heart once more.

"No, I will remain," she stated quite firmly, despite the quailing of her heart. "For Lady Matilda's sake, I must know if I am correct in my assumptions." She did not doubt for a moment that she had the right of it but still, the urge to remain present stayed with her. Lord Stratham kept her gaze for another moment, nodded, and then made to say something to Lord Brinsworth – only for the door to open and, with a broad smile and a laugh escaping her, Lady Kellingston stepped into the room.

The Duke of Abernyte stepped swiftly forward and closed the door behind the lady sharply, with Lady Kellingston starting violently as he did so. Her smile shattered and she looked wildly all about her before her gaze finally rested on Georgina. Georgina's stomach twisted as Lady Kellingston came a few steps closer to her, one hand outstretched. Her cheeks were pale, her eyes huge and

Georgina felt her own heart begin to cry out with sorrow and upset.

"Whatever is going on, Lady Georgina?" Lady Kellingston's voice was filled with a false confidence that did not leech into her expression. "I thought that there was a message waiting here for me and now I find that I am..." She looked all around again, her voice fading away. "I am surrounded."

Closing her eyes for a moment, Georgina drew in a deep breath and then spoke directly to the lady. She had not been asked to, had not even been encouraged to, but still, she felt that it was her duty now.

"Lady Kellingston," she said, aware of the slight tremble in her voice. "How fares your son?"

The change in Lady Kellingston's expression was instantaneous. Color drained from her, her skin going almost paper-like as she pressed both hands to her mouth. Shaking violently, she stared back into Georgina's eyes, before letting out a cry which shattered the silence that surrounded them all.

"You do not deny it, then." The Duke of Abernyte stepped forward, ignoring Lady Kellingston's distress, and speaking with such severity that Georgina could not help but start violently.

"Oh, Your Grace." Lady Kellingston did not look up, her hands now moving to cover her eyes as she spoke. "I – I cannot help but be relieved but still, what is to become of my son?" Her hands dropped away, and she looked up at him, leaving Georgina to frown, not at all sure of what Lady Kellingston meant in speaking about her relief. "Pray, do you know anything of him?"

The question itself did not seem to fit with what Georgina had suspected of Lady Kellingston, thinking to herself that she showed no upset or sorrow at being so discovered. Instead, there seemed to be nothing more than genuine desperation as to news of her son.

"Lady Kellingston, you do understand the severity of your actions?" Lord Brinsworth stepped forward out of the shadows, his face a mask as his eyes bored into the lady. "This is treason."

For a moment, Lady Kellingston stared at Lord Brinsworth, and then the next, she was swaying violently. It was as though she had only just realized what they knew, as though she had hoped that they had not the full truth but, in being told otherwise, now saw that she had no other recourse. Lord Stratham caught her before she fell, and the Duke helped the lady into a chair. Lady Kellingston's head was in her hands, and she let out a low moan, sending a shiver down Georgina's spine. Looking around the room, Georgina quickly spotted the brandy decanter in the corner and, ignoring the slight trembling of her own limbs, went to pour Lady Kellingston a small measure. Yes, the lady had done ill, but that did not mean that she did not deserve even the tiniest sympathy.

"Oh, Lady Georgina." Lady Kellingston grasped the glass with one hand and, with the other, pulled at Georgina's wrist. Her strength was rather more than Georgina had expected and Georgina found that she had no choice but to look into Lady Kellingston's eyes, her stomach twisting as she saw the fear held there.

"Lady Kellingston, whatever it is you have done, there are consequences for it," she said stiffly, not certain how else to react. "Lady Matilda will be well cared for. Lord Bulford will wed her. She will be given security and contentment – as much contentment as she can have, given the circum-stances."

Georgina made to pull her wrist away, but Lady Kellingston pulled at her all the more, seemingly quite desperate now to have Georgina listen to her.

"But you must tell her that I did not do it all willingly," the lady said, hoarsely, as tears began to spill from her eyes. "Whatever you tell her, promise me you will tell her that."

A frown pulled at Georgina's brow as she looked down into the pale face of Lady Kellingston and found herself uncertain of what she ought to say or do next. Doubt began to eat away at her mind, suddenly questioning whether all that she had thought of Lady Kellingston was, in fact, quite true.

"What do you mean, Lady Kellingston?" Lord Stratham came to stand beside Georgina, his hand snaking across the small of Georgina's back as Lady Kellingston continued to clutch her. "Do you imply that you had no choice?"

Lady Kellingston nodded, her jaw working furiously for a short while before she was able to answer. Georgina glanced up, seeing Lord Brinsworth and the Duke of Abernyte both wearing similar looks of confusion and doubt – and the truth began to dawn.

"They came to me," Lady Kellingston whispered, closing her eyes tightly as tears continued to slip down her cheeks. "They said that they had my son. Indeed, they even had a note from him and, despite my lack of willingness to believe it, I knew that it was written in his hand. Besides which," she continued, her head dropping forward for a few moments, "he wrote of one or two things which only Kellingston would have known."

"Who spoke to you?" Georgina asked, only for Lord Stratham to shake his head warningly. Now was not the time for such questions. Lady Kellingston had to be able to speak as she wished.

"They said that if I did not do as they asked, then they would... they would kill my son."

Her words echoed around the room, and it seemed to suddenly crackle with the shared awareness that came over them all. Georgina's heart began to pound furiously, her eyes widening with horror as Lady Kellingston continued.

"If I told another living soul, then my son would be killed," the lady continued, hopelessly. "I did not want to do what they asked, but what else could I do?" She spread her hands and looked up at Georgina, helplessly. "To be responsible for my own son's demise? No, I could not allow it. I begged my brother to do what he could to find Lord Kellingston but that was all that I spoke to him about – I revealed nothing to him of what had happened. But he could not find anything out about my son and thus, I was left with no other choice but to do as they asked."

Silence filled the room and Georgina closed her eyes, finding herself turning into the security of Lord Stratham's arms. She had been wrong. Yes, Lady Kellingston *was* the one who had been aiding the French, but it was not for her own selfish reasons, as Georgina had thought. Instead, it seemed that she had been forced into doing so without any way to escape from the expectations which had been laid upon her. In a way, Lady Kellingston had been in her own prison, forced to obey the demands of her gaolers without question or denial.

"You have been aiding the French but only out of necessity."

The Duke of Abernyte spoke slowly as Lady Kellingston began to nod, fresh tears beginning to pour down her cheeks. Georgina felt for her lace handkerchief and, pulling it from her pockets, pressed it into the lady's hands. Lady Kellingston took it at once, her whole body shaking with sobs. Georgina felt tears prick in her own eyes as she leaned back into Lord Stratham, hardly able to imagine the horror which had filled Lady Kellingston as she had fought to protect her son by betraying her country. The struggle, the dilemma, the guilt, and the loneliness must have been almost unbearable.

"I overheard you speak, Lord Stratham, and decided that I must leave London. I was so very afraid that my name would be divulged and that you would come for me without knowing the truth of it all." Lady Kellingston looked up at Lord Stratham, then her eyes strayed to Georgina's. "I did not realize that you had become aware of what I was doing, Lady Georgina." Her eyes closed for a moment. "Matilda –"

"Knows nothing," Georgina promised, quickly. "She is, I am afraid, on her way to Scotland." The tiniest of smiles caught her lips as Lady Kellingston looked up sharply. "She does not think so ill of Lord Bulford as you, it seems. She would not be kept from him." One shoulder lifted. "I expect to hear from her by the sennight's end."

Lady Kellingston's head dropped forward, and she covered her face with her hands. Georgina did not know what to do, wanting to go to the lady to comfort her and yet, at the same time, being held back by her own uncertainty. Glancing up into Lord Stratham's face, she saw him looking at the Duke of Abernyte, a dark expression on his face which was, much to her astonishment, being returned by a nod. Just what was it that the gentlemen now had planned for Lady Kellingston? Her heart tore painfully as she slipped one hand under his arm, intending to speak to him if she had to, to plead Lady Kellingston's case, to demand that they did not treat her as though she were a traitor. Yes, she had aided the French but, at the same time, she had not done so with any willingness.

"What do you know of the man following Lord Brinsworth, Lady Kellingston?" The Duke came forward and Lady Kellingston dropped her hands, daring to look up at the gentleman – only to drop her head again as she saw the expression on his face. "Why was he being followed?"

Georgina watched closely as Lady Kellingston shook her head.

"I was told only to write should I hear of any gentleman's return to London, gentlemen who might be of specific interest," she said, softly. "I heard of your return, Lord Stratham, and so I wrote of that. I then received a note stating all that you had done and was asked to write again should I see you in specific and frequent company of any one person."

Georgina felt Lord Stratham stiffen.

"Did you speak to my father of Lord Stratham and what you knew of him?" she asked, before Lord Stratham could say anything. "Is that how he knew so much of him?"

Lady Kellingston nodded but said nothing more.

"And therefore, once you saw that Lord Stratham was often in my company, you wrote, as you were required to do, to inform them of our friendship," the Duke finished, sounding all the more grave. "But what of Lord Brinsworth?"

A shuddering sigh came from Lady Kellingston's lips and, for a few moments, she did not speak. Eventually, with closed eyes and hands clasped tightly in her lap, she continued her explanation.

"Men always watch my comings and goings," she said, her voice breaking with unspoken emotion. "I do not know them nor who sends them, but they are always there. They do not care if I know who they are and what they are doing." A shudder shook her frame, and she closed her eyes momentarily. "It was all I could do to keep it from Matilda."

Georgina looked at Lord Stratham, seeing the lingering frown on his face and wondering if he felt anything akin to the sympathy which now poured into her own heart as she continued listening to Lady Kellingston. It was clear that she had been under a lot of strain, forced into that particular position by someone as yet unknown. Surely Lord Stratham could see that it was not deliberate on Lady Kellingston's part!

"I heard from Lady Buttars that Lord Brinsworth was returned to London from the war," Lady Kellingston continued, her voice still shaking. "Instead of writing, as I usually did, I spoke directly to one of the men who stand guard outside my house." One shoulder lifted. "I think I hoped that it would remove him and perhaps some others from my door for a short while and, whilst that certainly occurred, they were instantly replaced with others." Her face fell. "*He* is the one that followed you, Lord Brinsworth – although I do not think that he expected you to be so aware of him." A slight bitterness came into her voice. "They think that they are all the more powerful, all the more devious than any other. I am only sorry, Lady Georgina, that *you* were caught up in it all." Her eyes turned to Georgina and, despite her awareness of the severity of the situation, Georgina could not help but go to her. She took Lady Kellingston's outstretched hands in her own and pressed them hard.

"It was not your doing," she said, firmly. "It was unfortunate, that was all. I am, as you can see, quite unharmed." She gave Lady Kellingston a small smile, but this served only to have the lady dropping her head and beginning to cry once more. Desperate, Georgina looked over her shoulder at Lord Stratham but saw that he had moved to speak to the Duke of Abernyte and Lord Brinsworth. They stood clustered together a little away from Georgina and Lady Kellingston, speaking in low voices as they deliberated on what they had been told.

"I had no choice," Lady Kellingston whispered, brokenly. "No choice whatsoever. My son –"

"Who is it, Lady Kellingston, that you write to?" Lord Brinsworth interrupted, coming back towards them. "You say that you have been forced to do these treasonous things for fear that your son will, otherwise, be killed." He arched one eyebrow and Georgina immediately glared at him, a little frustrated by his lack of compassion. "Who is it that you write to? Who has threatened these things?"

Lady Kellingston shook her head.

"I do not know the names of anyone involved, save for one," she stated, lifting her head and, for the first time, Georgina saw her eyes free of tears and of fear. It was as though she had now determined that it was best to speak the truth without hesitation, given all that had been disclosed. "When I was first approached with news of my son, it was by two men only. Men who represented the cruel and cold-hearted gentleman who demanded such things of me. That has always been the case, for it is quite obvious that they do not want me to know the names and the like of those who are so vehemently against supporting the Crown."

"To do so would be dangerous, for then you might have some leverage," Lord Stratham replied, coming back to stand beside Georgina. "But you say that you know one name?"

Lady Kellingston nodded, a slight hesitancy about her lips as she replied.

"I – I cannot be quite certain, but I did overhear a name.

When I spoke to the man outside my house about Lord Brinsworth's return, he, thereafter, mentioned to another man that their master would have to know of it at once." She swallowed hard, still visibly trembling. "I believe – although I am not, at present, able to say for certain – that the name of Lord Jeffries was mentioned."

A tightness grasped Georgina's heart and she gasped in shock, suddenly recalling how Lady Kellingston had attempted to discourage Georgina's mother from pushing that gentleman towards her.

"Lord Jeffries, eh?" the Duke murmured, one eyebrow lifting as he looked first at Lord Brinsworth and then at Lord Stratham. "Well, Lady Kellingston, we shall have to do a little probing and the like, but if it *is* as you say, then I think we can offer you a little... grace."

Relief swamped Georgina as the lady rose from her chair, albeit somewhat unsteadily, and looked back at the Duke.

"Your hand was forced," Lord Stratham said, quietly. "I cannot say that there will be no consequences to bear, Lady Kellingston, but it appears that you are not deliberately fighting against the Crown."

"No, I am not," Lady Kellingston replied, her voice thin but a tiny pinch of color back in her cheeks. "But I am torn between my duty to my son and my duty to the Crown. Tell me, Lord Stratham." Her eyes went to Georgina. "If Lady Georgina had been captured and her life was at stake, then just what would you do to make certain of her safety?"

There was no immediate answer, for Lord Stratham opened his mouth to speak, only to close it again as he looked back at Georgina for a long moment.

"As I have said," he answered, eventually, "there will be consequences, certainly, but there will be nothing of great severity. Indeed, I am certain that we will do all we can to help you find your son, Lady Kellingston. I pray that he will be returned to you."

Lord Brinsworth cleared his throat before going to the door. Opening it, he glanced out into the hallway for a moment before nodding to the Duke.

"Allow me to return you to the drawing-room, Lady Kellingston," the Duke murmured, offering his arm to the lady. "A fortifying drink, I believe, will be of great aid. There is more that will be required of you yet, certainly, but for the moment, rest in the knowledge that you are no longer alone with this burden."

"We are here to help you," Georgina found herself saying, ignoring the surprise which shot across Lord Stratham's face. "Pray take heart, Lady Kellingston." She smiled at the lady as she threw a glance back towards her. "And prepare for the news of Lady Matilda's elopement!"

A small, dry laugh escaped from Lady Kellingston, her lips in a sad smile as the Duke led her from the room. Lord Brinsworth followed, and Georgina closed her eyes, her shoulders drooping as she allowed relief to flood her. Lady Kellingston was not what she had believed her to be. Yes, the truth was dreadful and certainly a good deal more injurious in some ways, but, at the very least, Lady Kellingston was not a willing party to all that had taken place. She was glad that the truth was now known and that the three gentlemen could now turn their interest towards Lord Jeffries.

And perhaps she, finally, could turn her thoughts towards her own heart.

EPILOGUE

Frederick took in Lady Georgina, seeing the way that her shoulders slumped and her head bowed low. For himself, he was very glad that the truth was known to them all and that, finally, they had someone to investigate a little further, now they knew that Lord Jeffries was not everything which he made himself out to be. His heart ached for Lady Georgina, seeing her so weary and perhaps a little forlorn, now that the matter with Lady Kellingston had been brought to a close. Aware that they were quite alone, Frederick chose to use their solitude to speak as he had long hoped to do.

"Lady Georgina," he murmured, making to step closer to her, only for Lady Georgina's head to lift, her eyes to brighten, and for her to practically fling herself into his arms. Frederick caught his breath as he held her tightly, a little astonished at her exuberance, but overcome with happiness that she had turned to him for comfort. Holding her close, he closed his eyes and drew in a long breath, wanting now to speak to her of his own emotions.

"You have shown such great courage and had such marvelous insight that I am quite in awe of you, Lady Georgina," he said, softly into her ear. "I do not think I know another quite like you."

She lifted her head and looked up into his face, her hands lingering about his neck.

"You are not angry with me?"

"Angry?" He was a little surprised at the suggestion. "Why should I be so?"

Lady Georgina shrugged, looking a little abashed.

"I have been very forward," she replied, quietly. "Bold and even perhaps a little arrogant in my insistence." Her eyes darted back to his for just a moment. "I fear that you will think ill of me."

He shook his head.

"I am only grateful that you *were* so determined, else we might never have discovered the truth," he told her, honestly. "Lady Georgina, *you* have brought this about. You should feel not only a sense of relief but also of pride." Lifting his hand from her waist, he brushed it down her cheek. "I know that I think all the more highly of you, given all that you have done and achieved."

Her smile was a trifle uncertain but the more their gaze held, the brighter it became.

"Allow me to be bold one more time," she said, after a few moments. "Is there anything *more* within your heart for me, Lord Stratham?"

Her cheeks colored gently as she waited for his answer, making Frederick chuckle.

"I am grateful for your understanding and willingness to forgive my first actions," he replied, teasingly, referring to when he had first told her the truth of his reason for their acquaintance. "Is that what you mean?" Seeing her blush and look away, Frederick forced himself to be serious. "In truth, Lady Georgina, I find myself so desperately in love with you that I do not think it can be hidden for any longer." He saw the sparkle in her eyes and felt his heart lift with both gladness and relief. "Your mother may not wish you to wed a scarred gentleman, but I will ask for your hand, Lady Georgina, regardless. That is," he continued, hoping that she would be just as willing to consider their future as he, "if you would be willing to even consider such a thing."

"Consider it?" She laughed, her hands still about his neck, her fingers brushing through his hair. "Lord Stratham, you must know by now that I am not at all inclined towards doing as my mother wishes. I am often very eager to do the precise opposite!" Another gentle laugh escaped her as she pulled herself closer to him, with Frederick almost overcome with the urge to kiss her. "I have come to find that my love for you grows with almost every moment that passes, Lord Stratham," she finished, now growing suddenly serious. "Whenever you wish to ask me, be assured of my answer."

Frederick tried to resist the urge to lower his head, but Lady Georgina had no such hesitation. Reaching up on tiptoe, she pressed her lips to his and Frederick found himself kissing her with all the passion and love that had been buried for so long within his heart. His arms held her tightly, their hearts slowly beginning to beat as one.

Their future was bright, and Frederick could hardly believe his luck. A scarred gentleman, brought back from war, had finally found happiness and a love that nothing – not even the disapproval of Lady Kingham – could ever take away.

"I love you, Georgina," he whispered against her lips, as she looked up into his eyes.

"And I love you," came her sweet and gentle reply.

A HAPPY Ever After for two deserving people, Frederick and Georgina! If you missed the first book in this series, please check out To Trust a Viscount

MY DEAR READER

Thank you for reading and supporting my books! I hope this story brought you some escape from the real world into the always captivating Regency world. A good story, especially one with a happy ending, just brightens your day and makes you feel good! If you enjoyed the book, would you leave a review on Amazon? Reviews are always appreciated.

Below is a complete list of all my books! Why not click and see if one of them can keep you entertained for a few hours?

The Duke's Daughters Series
The Duke's Daughters: A Sweet Regency Romance Boxset
A Rogue for a Lady
My Restless Earl
Rescued by an Earl
In the Arms of an Earl
The Reluctant Marquess (Prequel)

A Smithfield Market Regency Romance
The Smithfield Market Romances: A Sweet Regency
Romance Boxset
The Rogue's Flower
Saved by the Scoundrel
Mending the Duke
The Baron's Malady

Second Chance Regency Romance
Loving the Scarred Soldier
Second Chance for Love
A Family of her Own
A Spinster No More

Soldiers and Sweethearts
To Trust a Viscount
Whispers of the Heart
Dare to Love a Marquess

Christmas Stories
Love and Christmas Wishes: Three Regency Romance
Novellas
A Family for Christmas
Mistletoe Magic: A Regency Romance
Heart, Homes & Holidays: A Sweet Romance Anthology

Happy Reading!

All my love,

Rose

A SNEAK PEAK OF TO TRUST
A VISCOUNT

CHAPTER ONE

"*Y*ou must return to England."

"No." Daniel shook his head hard and immediately winced at the pain that shot through his shoulder and down his arm. Grimacing, he tried to ignore the fire that seemed to burn into his very bones. "I can still be of assistance here."

"You cannot." The Marquess of Stratham put one hand on Daniel's shoulder – his good shoulder – and looked steadily into his eyes. "You need to return home."

It went against every instinct that Daniel had. The war was here. The fighting was here. The defense of his country was here. Yes, he had been injured but surely that did not mean he simply had to turn tail and go home? Desperately, he looked back at his friend and prayed silently that the Marquess would see the extent of his determination and offer him another alternative, but as the minutes ticked by slowly, Daniel began to realize that it was not to be.

"I am sorry."

Dropping his head, Daniel let out a long sigh but did not allow any further protestations to pass his lips. The decision had been made, it seemed, and he could no longer fight against Napoleon's forces. Had he not been forced from his horse, had he not fallen so very badly, then he might now be back in his position and doing all he could to prevent the French from proceeding. Instead, it seemed, he was to return to England and to know nothing more about what was being done here. Whilst Daniel was grateful for his life of comfort, it did not seem so much of a comfort any longer. To return to his estate and to that particular way of life did not hold any sort of delight for him. Instead, he felt himself burdened. His heart was heavy with grief, anger, and frustration.

Someone stepped inside, handing the Marquess a note, which he took at once. Daniel did not look up, keeping his head bowed and forcing himself to breathe at a steady pace so that he would not give in to the despair that continued to snap at his heels.

"My goodness...."

In an instant, Daniel's head shot up and he looked eagerly back at his friend. His heart was pounding quickly, his good hand curling into a tight fist as he saw the Marquess look from the letter to Daniel and back to the letter again.

"Well," the Marquess said, his chin lifting just a little and a brightness coming into his eyes. "I was very sorry to have to send you home to recover, but it seems now that fate is calling you back to England." Leaning forward, he handed Daniel the note. "You are now the Viscount Harrogate."

All of the air seemed to be pulled from around Daniel as he held the note in his hand and read it carefully. He could hardly believe what he was seeing, for the few short lines informed him that his uncle had, unfortunately, passed away and that he was now the new bearer of the title of Viscount. His uncle was not someone that Daniel had ever been particularly well acquainted with and, whilst he had known that he would inherit the title should anything happen to his uncle before his uncle produced an heir, Daniel had never considered it a near possibility. His uncle had not been anywhere near his dotage and, having only recently married, Daniel had expected an heir to be produced in the next few years.

"How – how did he die?" he muttered to himself, still trying to take in this news. "And there is no heir?"

"It seems there is not," the Marquess replied, one shoulder lifting as though to say that this was not a matter of any great importance. "Well, well! A Viscount!" He chuckled, then leaned forward and looked steadily at Daniel. "How would you feel about making your way to London, Viscount Harrogate?"

It was as though a great and heavy fog now pushed itself forward, flowing over Daniel and making him struggle to see or hear the Marquess clearly.

"To London?" he repeated, a little unsteadily. "For what purpose?"

The Marquess chuckled.

"For the Season!" he exclaimed, as though that was all that Daniel ought to be thinking about. "You must go to London for the Season and find yourself a pretty young lady to be your wife, given that you will now have to make certain to produce an heir!"

Daniel swallowed hard, feeling dust in his throat as he tried to make sense of what the Marquess was saying.

"The Duke of Abernyte will be there," the Marquess continued, the smile dropping from his face as he leaned forward in his chair, fixing Daniel with a serious look. "There is a message that I must relay to him."

"And you wish me to do it?" Daniel asked, still a little overwhelmed. "All because I am now a Viscount?" A sense of unfairness began to wash over him. "I could not have done it when I was an untitled gentleman, only a few minutes ago?"

Again, the Marquess shrugged.

"I must take my opportunities where they present themselves," he replied, calmly. "As an untitled gentleman, you would not be in the same social circle as the Duke and might arouse suspicion should you attempt to gain his company. However, as a Viscount, there will be nothing at all to concern anyone."

He sat back in his chair and smiled, leaving Daniel to blink rapidly as he fought to put everything the Marquess had said into clear, coherent order.

"You wish me to attend the London Season, to find the Duke, and to relay a message to him," he said, speaking each word with great deliberation and slowness. "The message no doubt relates to war matters."

The Marquess of Stratham nodded, his eyes still grave.

"That is it, precisely."

"And what is this message to be?"

Clearing his throat, the Marquess sat up straight in his chair.

"There are a few concerning matters as regards an impending invasion," he said, sending a jolt of shock through Daniel's frame. "The southeast coast is the expected destination of our enemy, and it is being prepared for battle. However," he continued, as Daniel hung on every word which was being spoken, "we expect there to be a few of the French already making their way into our country as spies, so that they might report on all that is taking place. Some may even attempt to become connected with those in high places, with those who consider, debate, and decide what we are to do next."

"Such as the Duke," Daniel interrupted, seeing the Marquess nod. Daniel knew that the Duke of Abernyte had been involved in the war effort although he was not privy to the role that the Duke might have played. "What is it that I must tell him?"

The Marquess grinned, the severe look in his eyes fading in an instant.

"You will go then?"

Daniel nodded.

"Yes, I will."

"Capital." The Marquess' smile remained fixed. "Then I will write my message for the Duke, and will rest assured that you will give it only to him." His eyes fixed to Daniel's. "I beg of you to keep the seal unbroken, that you will not look inside or read the note under any circumstance."

"I will not."

Daniel lifted his chin, knowing that the Marquess of Stratham – and indeed, the country itself – required his allegiance.

"It is not that I do not trust you, but only that the words contained within will be solely for the Duke's eyes," the Marquess finished, as Daniel nodded. "It may be that what I write will be proven incorrect, although, given what I have heard...." He trailed off and shook his head. "Very good. I will write it this very hour."

"I will hand it directly to the Duke of Abernyte, just as soon as I return to London," Daniel promised. "You have my word."

CHAPTER TWO

"*A*re you looking forward to this evening's ball?"

Sarah smiled a little ruefully as she looked back at her cousin, wondering when Miss Florence Addington would stop talking incessantly about the ball which they were to attend that evening. She did not even need to answer her cousin's question, for the lady was already continuing to speak at length about what she herself would be wearing this evening, what color her gown was, and the various trimmings that had been sewn onto it. Sarah, who had heard all of this many times before, stifled a yawn and picked up her book. Attempting to read it proved difficult, however, for Florence was quite insistent that they discuss which gentlemen might be present, and whether or not Sarah had any intention of dancing the waltz – for even if she was permitted, it was still entirely her decision as to whether or not she stood up with anyone.

"I am not sure," Sarah replied, still trying to read her book, but finding herself becoming so frustrated with Florence's inane chatter that she simply could not concentrate on the words which were before her. Sighing heavily, she set her book down and let out a long breath of frustration, which she did not let Florence see. They had only just made their come out and, whilst Sarah had to admit that she was very eager indeed for this evening's event, she was not quite as excited as her cousin! She was quite content to know that yes, there would be gentlemen present and yes, there would be dancing also, but felt no need to continually – and audibly – discuss whether or not certain people would be present and, if so, what they might be wearing.

"The Duke is to attend, is he not?"

Sarah looked back at Florence and shook her head.

"My cousin is not to attend, no," she replied, aware of the small ball of tension that began to roll itself around her stomach. "He is not in London at present, I believe."

The Duke of Abernyte was her cousin on her mother's side, whilst Florence was her cousin on her father's side – although this did not prevent Florence from taking a great deal of interest in the Duke! That was to be expected, however, for the Duke of Abernyte was unwed and unattached at present, and every mother in the *ton* silently prayed, no doubt, that their daughter would be the one to catch his eye. The gentleman needed an heir and thus, there were many expectant and eager hearts waiting for his return to London.

And it seemed that Florence was one of them.

"Oh." Florence's face fell immediately, clearly disappointed that the Duke was not going to be in attendance that evening. "I had hoped he might dance with me, given that he is practically my own relation!" She laughed and Sarah shook her head, knowing that there was no real connection between Florence and the Duke but finding herself quite unable to argue with her cousin. "Do you know if he is to come to London at all this Season?"

Sarah shook her head.

"I could not say." Her fingers twisted together as she prayed silently that Florence would think of speaking of someone else instead, finding herself growing very weary of the conversation indeed. "Tell me, what will your mother be dressed in this evening?"

This, she realized with relief, was precisely what she ought to have said at the beginning of the conversation about the Duke, for it distracted Florence almost immediately. She quickly began to describe her mother's gown and all the particular trimmings which were to go with it. Sarah let out a long, slow breath, although she nodded and smiled and agreed with all that was being said in the interim.

"Ah, there you are." Her mother walked into the room and interrupted their conversation, forcing Sarah to set aside her book entirely for the present. "Lady Flenshaw will return soon, my dear," she continued, speaking to Florence. "Your mother has decided that her gloves are in need of replacement and has taken the carriage to Bond Street so that she might purchase a new pair for this evening."

A quick glance told Sarah exactly what her mother thought of Lady Flenshaw's insistence that her gloves would not do. She hid a smile and saw the twinkle that sparkled in her mother's eye in return. Lady Flenshaw – being Lady Blackwell's sister – was very much like Florence in her manner. Whilst Sarah had to endure Florence's conversation about the same things over and over again, she was fully aware that her mother had to endure the very same thing with Lady Flenshaw. As if to emphasize that fact, Florence had launched into a discussion of the merits of gloves, immediately.

"Sarah, do go and ring for tea," her mother said, interrupting Florence's flow of words for a moment. "I think we will require a little more refreshment before my sister returns to the house."

Sarah smiled at her mother gratefully, rose, and said she would take a short turn about the house before she did so, stating that she was sure that Florence would keep her mother engaged. Lady Blackwell laughed and flapped one hand at Sarah as if to chase her out of the room, and Sarah went quickly, glad indeed of a few minute's respite.

She had been sitting with Florence for some time and it felt good to be able to walk for a short while. Stopping a maid, she requested a new tea tray to be sent to the drawing-room and then continued on her way. She climbed the stairs, walked into her bed-chamber, and sat down on the bed, letting out a sigh of relief as she did so.

Her eyes fell on the gown that she was to wear this evening, which had already been laid out for her. A small swirl of excitement ran through her as she thought about the dancing and the conversation which would take place. Despite Florence's ongoing conversation about it, Sarah had to admit that she was a *little* excited. Rising to her feet, she brushed one hand down the fall of the gown, gently sighing with contentment. This was to be her first Season and, having already been presented, she would go into society with the express purpose of finding a suitable match.

Her father, the Viscount, was very wealthy indeed and had promised her an excellent dowry, but Sarah felt herself a little less than inclined to be sold off to whichever gentleman thought her dowry good enough! Instead, she considered, tilting her head just a little as she looked at the gown, she wanted nothing more than to be wed to a gentleman who cared for her and truly considered her. She did not think that to be in love was something that she ought to pursue, but neither would Sarah settle for a gentleman who only cared about the amount of coin he would receive upon their marrying!

"The tea tray has been delivered to the drawing-room, my Lady."

Pulled from her thoughts, Sarah turned around and thanked the maid. Taking a deep breath, she made her way out of the bedroom and back down the stairs, steeling herself for another hour or so of enduring Florence's inane chatter about this evening.

"He has gone to Bath on an urgent matter, I believe, but will return within a few days."

Upon hearing her father's voice echoing up from the hallway below, Sarah stopped immediately, only two steps down the stairs.

"What have you heard from him?"

There was a moment's pause.

"Very little," her father responded to whomever else was speaking. "The Duke does not inform me of a great deal, although, of course, I am glad to do what I can. I am too old and infirm to have any dealings with the war itself, save for taking a message here and there when I can, or contributing in a monetary way."

"For which I am sure there is a good deal of gratitude," the other voice said. "But I must find the Duke of Abernyte at once. There is something I must give to him."

Sarah turned her head and looked behind her, wondering if she ought to return to her bed-chamber and wait until her father had finished his conversation, only for the sound of footsteps to rise towards her.

"If I find out where His Grace is, I shall tell you at

once," she heard her father say, his voice a little more commanding now. "You have my word."

This did not seem to satisfy the other gentleman, for a heavy sigh followed her father's words, and only after some moments did she hear both men walking towards the front door of the house, and the other man making an almost grudging final remark.

"I thank you. It seems I must away to Bath, and hope to find him."

Sarah quickly made her way down the rest of the stairs hoping to return to the drawing-room before her father saw her but, unfortunately, as she proceeded to the last few steps, her father reappeared. He looked a little surprised upon seeing her, only for his brows to knot together. Sarah flushed at once. She had never been able to hide anything from anyone, for her expression always told the truth.

"Sarah." Her father lifted one eyebrow. "I fear you have overheard some of my conversation with Baron Northwood."

"I – I did, father," Sarah admitted, unwilling to even consider lying to him. "I did not mean to! I–"

"I thought you were in the drawing-room with your mother and Florence," her father interrupted, although his voice did not rise, and he did not appear to be angry with her. "Else I would not have finished my conversation with him out in the hall." His lips twisted for a moment, and he shook his head, looking away from her as he frowned. "Lord Northwood was most insistent."

"He needs to find the Duke?" Sarah asked, unable to help herself. "Why should he wish to do so with such urgency?"

Her eyes rounded in surprise as her father shook his head, grimacing as he did so.

"The Duke is involved with our efforts in the war against France," he told her plainly. "He and I have discussed matters upon occasion, but I do not always know the particulars. However," he continued, coming a small step closer to her and dropping his voice so that he spoke in low, quiet tones, "the Duke *has* gone away on business – although some of it will be to do with Napoleon's forces, I am certain of it – but he begged me not to speak of it to anyone."

Sarah blinked in surprise.

"But I heard you tell Lord Northwood that the Duke was gone to Bath!" she exclaimed, as her father quickly shook his head. "That was not the truth, then?"

"No, of course, it was not," her father replied, chuckling quietly. "He is gone to the coast." His brow furrowed and his smile slipped. "There is rumor of a French invasion, and the Duke is gone to make certain it does not occur, although he fears that there may be some within our own circle who are eager for such a thing to take place."

This was not the first time that Lord Blackwell had spoken to Sarah about such things. He had, at one time, been in the militia and, since then, had always been involved in one way or the other when it came to defending the Crown. She had an interest in the war and wanted to know what was occurring at any one time, simply so that she did not become a simpleton who cared only about gowns and balls. Her father, after some reluctance, had been honest with her and, since then, had been more than willing to discuss what he knew or what he was involved in at present, where that was permissible. The Duke, when Sarah had last seen him, had also spoken to her about the war against the French forces, and Sarah had been glad to know of what was taking place. It gave her a good deal to both consider and pray about.

"I am only a little acquainted with Baron Northwood and I certainly have no willingness to speak to him about any particular matter as regards the Duke's whereabouts," her father continued, giving a small, abrupt shake of his head as though to make quite clear how little he thought of Baron Northwood's request. "That does not mean that I believe that there is anything untoward in the Baron's motivations, however. It is only that I am doing as my nephew asked and keeping the matter entirely to myself." One finger waggled itself at Sarah. "You will not tell anyone anything of this, Sarah."

"Of course I will not!"

Sarah was a little affronted, thinking that her father did not consider her trustworthy but, instead, the Viscount only chuckled, shattering that perception immediately.

"I know that you are always able to be trusted," the Viscount said, reaching out to take Sarah's hand for a moment. "I am only teasing you, my dear." This was followed by a small frown, his smile fading. "Although you are aware of the seriousness of all that the Duke is involved in."

Sarah nodded, pressing her father's hand in return.

"I am, father," she said, seriously. "I will not say a word. I do hope that the Duke is successful in whatever endeavors he is undertaking at present. An invasion to England's shores would be a grave matter indeed."

"I too pray that he finds success," came the reply, which was followed by her father rubbing at his forehead, his lips pressing tightly together for a moment. "We must not forget the significance of what is happening far from our shores, my dear. There is so much that might yet take place."

Swallowing hard, Sarah took a moment before she replied, feeling a fluttering of fear in her heart as she considered the war and all that could happen, should England's forces be unsuccessful in their attempted defeat of the French.

"Let us pray that they will have nothing but triumph, father," she said softly, seeing her father's eyes catch hers for just a moment and then hurry away again, as though he did not want to look into her face and give her news that would bring her nothing but distress. "I am certain that they will defeat Napoleon and his forces."

Her father smiled tightly but it did not reach his eyes. Instead, he merely patted her arm and stepped away, leaving Sarah standing alone in the hallway. Her brow furrowed for a moment as she watched him return to his study, feeling greatly unsettled. Drawing in a deep breath, she closed her eyes and let it out again slowly, calming herself as she did so. She had no need to worry, as yet.

"I am to have another new gown for...."

Florence's excited exclamations floated into the hallway and Sarah allowed herself a small, rueful smile. Rather than thinking about the war, Napoleon, and the like, she had now to concentrate on an entirely different matter – the upcoming ball and all that came with it. Allowing a gentle peace to wrap around her heart, Sarah made her way back into the drawing-room and was instantly caught up in the conversation once more, leaving all thought of the Duke and the war far, far behind.

"AND THIS MUST BE YOUR DAUGHTER."

Sarah blushed as the gentleman eyed her openly, his gaze sweeping from the top of her head all the way down to her feet and back again. Heat seared her, but it was not the pleasant sort. Instead, she found herself a little disgusted by the fellow, and, much to her relief, her mother appeared to feel the same.

"Yes, this is my daughter," Lady Blackwell replied, swiftly making the introductions. "Unfortunately, Lord Sumption, she is already engaged for a dance at present so you must excuse us." She bobbed a quick curtsy and Sarah followed suit, relieved when they stepped away from him. "Lord Sumption is not at all the sort of gentleman I should like you to acquaint yourself with, my dear," Lady Blackwell hissed as they walked away. "I did not like the way that he stared at you!"

"Nor did I," Sarah admitted, feeling a trifle despondent. They had been at the ball for an hour now and, whilst she had many names on her dance card, none of the gentlemen had encouraged even the smallest flicker of interest in her. "I should not have liked to dance with him."

Lady Blackwell tutted – not at Sarah's admission but rather at the thought that Lord Sumption would wish to stand up with Sarah – and lifted her chin a little more.

"You have many acceptable gentlemen on your card," she stated, patting Sarah's hand in a reassuring manner. "This is only the first ball of many for this Season. I am sure that, in a sennight or so, you will have many more gentlemen eager for your company and your hand."

Sarah smiled, looking over at her mother as they made their way as far from Lord Sumption as possible. She made to say something, only for Florence to appear, waving at her furiously from a short distance away. Sarah watched as her cousin said something to her mother and to the gentleman with her, and then hurried over to where Sarah and her mother stood. For whatever reason, the gentleman came with her.

"Oh, is this not just a magnificent evening!" Florence exclaimed, as Sarah nodded and smiled, whilst allowing her eyes to glance at the gentleman beside Florence now and again. "My dance card is quite full! I could not believe it! When Lord Tucker asked if I could stand up with him, I accepted wholeheartedly and handed him my card, only for him to say that it was quite full!"

She trilled a laugh and Sarah felt her smile freeze in place, feeling a little embarrassed for her cousin's sake. On top of which, Florence had not introduced this gentleman to her or her mother, meaning that he stood, quite silently, next to Florence as she spoke.

"My dear child," Lady Blackwell began, interrupting Florence and bringing the torrent of words to a close for a short respite. "Might you wish to introduce us?"

She looked pointedly at the gentleman and Florence stopped speaking suddenly, looking over at him as though she had forgotten about him entirely.

"Oh, yes of course!" she cried, waving a hand as though to say the fact that she had forgotten to do so was of little importance. "Do forgive me." She laughed and patted the gentleman's arm in a most improper fashion. "This is Viscount Harrogate." She laughed again, this time slapping the Viscount's arm. "I should say, he is the *new* Viscount Harrogate, for he has only just taken the title!"

"Good evening," Sarah said hastily, wanting to interrupt so that her cousin could not say more to embarrass either herself or Viscount Harrogate. "I do hope that you are enjoying this evening, Lord Harrogate."

She bobbed a curtsey and looked hard at her cousin, waiting for Florence to complete the introductions. It took Lord Harrogate clearing his throat before Florence realized what she had not done.

"Oh, and this is my aunt, Viscountess Blackwell, and her daughter – and my cousin – Miss Sarah Graham."

"I am very glad to make your acquaintance." The gentleman bowed and then turned to Sarah's mother. "Lady Blackwell, I believe I have already been introduced to your husband earlier this evening, in the card room."

Lady Blackwell chuckled, her eyes twinkling.

"Yes, that is most likely where you would find him," she replied, making Sarah blush a little with her mother's frankness. "He finds himself most disinclined to balls, but if there is to be a game of cards then he will make certain to attend with us!"

"I quite understand," came the reply, although this was swiftly interrupted by Florence.

"Not that you are of such a mind, Lord Harrogate," she said, teasingly, her eyes bright as she practically bounced on the spot as she spoke. "You are to dance with me soon, I believe!"

"Yes, indeed," Lord Harrogate replied, although Sarah noticed that his smile appeared a little weary, for his eyes did not quite hold the same delight. She considered him carefully, taking in his stocky frame, his broad shoulders, and the square jaw. His blue eyes were bright but did not gleam with happiness and, whilst his dark hair was neat, it brushed across his forehead and hugged low to his brows. From her assessment, Sarah considered him to be a somewhat serious individual, who was, despite his willingness, perhaps a little less inclined to dancing than Florence considered him!

"Ah, Miss Graham!"

Sarah turned, just in time to see Lord Sumption approach them, his eyes gleaming.

"I thought you were to dance!" he exclaimed, gesturing to Lord Harrogate. "But it seems that the gentleman is already engaged."

This was an easy assumption to make given the way that Florence's hand now pressed on Lord Harrogate's arm, leaving Sarah struggling to know how to respond. She wanted nothing more than to say that she was, in fact, engaged for the first dance but the truth was, she had no excuse. Glancing across at her mother with a somewhat desperate look in her eyes, Sarah forced a smile and looked back at Lord Sumption. He was, once more, studying her with that somewhat licentious eye and Sarah flushed with embarrassment.

"Lord Sumption," she began, slowly, "you find me –"

"You find Miss Graham already engaged for this dance, I am afraid!"

Lord Harrogate interrupted their discussion with a small smile and a shrug, stepping away from Florence who appeared to be instantly upset at such news. Her brow furrowed, her mouth opened in protest – but Lady Blackwell came to stand by her, her hand reaching to grasp Florence's, who, at such a reaction, remained quite silent.

"Yes," Sarah stammered, throwing a quick glance towards Lord Harrogate who, whilst not smiling, had lifted his chin and given Lord Sumption a firm look which dared him to protest. "I am to dance with Lord Harrogate, Lord Sumption."

Just as she spoke, the musicians began to play as if they had waited precisely for that particular moment to begin, and Sarah felt a swell of relief when Lord Sumption stepped back. His face had shifted into a most displeased expression, with his lips twisted and his eyes narrowed, but there was nothing that he could do. Lord Harrogate looked to Sarah, smiled, and offered her his arm, which she accepted at once.

"I am so very grateful, Lord Harrogate," she murmured, as they quickly stepped away. "Lord Sumption is –"

"Lord Sumption is not a gentleman worthy of your consideration, nor your company, Miss Graham," he interrupted, although she did not mind it. "I have been in London only a fortnight and even I am aware that he is not a gentleman suitable for *any* young lady's company."

Sarah smiled up at him, thinking that he had proven himself to be a very considerate gentleman already.

"I do not know Lord Sumption at all, I confess," she replied, as they quickly joined the set. "However, I believe that I was able to make a good estimation of his character in only the first few minutes of our conversation this evening!"

"I do hope that your cousin will not be much put out," Lord Harrogate murmured, bowing as the dance began. "I hope that she will understand."

"I am quite certain she will," Sarah replied, although without much confidence in the matter. Her mother, she prayed, would explain the situation to Florence, but Sarah was quite sure that her cousin would be deeply disappointed to have had the dance stolen from her. "Thank you again, Lord Harrogate, you have quite saved me."

This time, his smile lit up his face and Sarah caught her breath at the brightness that came into his blue eyes.

"But of course," he said as they took their places in the line. He offered her his hand and waited for a moment for her to take it before they began to move through the steps of the dance in perfect synchronization with the other couples.

IT WAS a good thing Lord Harrogate was there when Sarah needed him! Check out the rest of the story in the Kindle Store to find out what happens next! To Trust a Viscount

JOIN MY MAILING LIST

Sign up for my newsletter to stay up to date on new releases, contests, giveaways, freebies, and deals!

Free book with signup!

Facebook Giveaways! Books and Amazon gift cards! Join me on Facebook: https://www. facebook.com/rosepearsonauthor

Website: www.RosePearsonAuthor.com

Follow me on Goodreads: Author Page

You can also follow me on Bookbub! Click on the picture below – see the Follow button?